"The Salamander King"

Book Six: *"Ohhhhh….My"*

A Continuation of Books One through Five

Editing/Formatting by Melanie Lopata,

Get It Write (www.getitwritepublishing.company)

Contact the Author via email: perkinsphoto7@aol.com

or mail: 82 Lincoln Street, Bath, Maine 04530

See Newton's Pond Map on the last page

Acknowledgements & Inspirations

Sandra Fish, for her insightful and cute ideas that led to the alligator, football, skunk and bunny segments in this book. It was really fun to hear her ideas and incorporate them into the ongoing story line of which she is also very knowledgeable.

Judy Gorey, RIP my dear old friend, who helped me in so many ways and continuously beat all us guys when we took our morning ten mile bicycle rides at Griffith Park in Los Angeles! She would have made a great wild animal rescue rehabber, so here she is in book six.

Smart, tenacious and loving, Linda Hollowood Benedict, my first cousin, makes a wonderful great horned owl. Her owl hubby is named James. Seeing how Linda's dad Hugh and her mom Bernice are the majestic bald eagles in Lake Tear of the Clouds, I thought it was prudent to keep them all in the raptor family.

My old friend Mike Fermil, who is the inspiration behind the Mike's Exotic Pet Store owner, comes back in the next book.

`I worked with Ben Peterson at my last real job and thought he would make a great snapping turtle, and he does as Ben.

Janis Benson Gillespie, Marty-Bull and the entire Bull family, Justin Thomas, Phil O'Donnell, Shane Rector, Carole Lombardi, Aunt Bernice and Uncle Hugh, Nancy Perkins McKee and family, Greg and Gayle Perkins, Chelsey Minor, the Gardner family, Joel and Christie Sweet, Peggy MacKellar, Barb Gokey Perkins and to all my relatives, friends and scholars who continuously assist me in this really enjoyable and meaningful writing experience.

All the small schools, elementary school teachers and librarians who have embraced the story, found it important, and wanted to share it with their children.

And…to whomever (?) at the local Bath, Maine YMCA that is making my five donated books disappear off, and reappear on, the book shelves, enjoy!

Dibyoshree Sarkar for her relentless effort, hard work and amazing talent to make the illustrations as wonderful as they are.

And last, but certainly not least, to Melanie Lopata for her brilliant and concise editing and formatting skills. And there she is, hard at work, hammering the reprobate author's manuscripts into ones that are English Dept. approved and school-ready!

Editing/Formatting by Melanie Lopata,

Get It Write (www.getitwritepublishing.company)

Table of Contents

Chapter One

"Come…Come Join Us!"

At Newton's home by the pond in Lake Luzerne, the beavers all give each other happy looks, and then Marty-Bull says to Grandpa, "My family is very excited to meet my folks, and for me, getting back to Lake Tear is going to be very special indeed. Lots of old friends."

"It's been over sixty years since I have seen Hugh and Bernice," adds Grandpa Lynn, who envisions the time he waved goodbye to the eagles and Lake Tear of the Clouds those many years ago.

"This is going to be wonderful," Janine says as Newton smiles at his new love that he waited such a long time to find..

"Oh, I can't wait for you to meet all our friends!" exalts Edie to Janine.

"All of this is wonderful, thanks to our human family," says Fred.

"You could not be more welcome, "Grandpa Lynn replies.

Back on the road in the Buick LeSabre, Grace says to her dad, "Well, that was a great idea, Dad. They trust us, as they should. No reason not to. We love them, and they know it."

Grandpa smiles at his daughter and says, "Oh, and Becky, bring along that low-dose sedative, just in case." Grace smiles back and winks at Becky.

"Going camping...with Grandpa, the newt and beaver families. Alright!", Wayne says excitedly. Becky, in the back seat with Wayne and Grace, does a happy dance with her arms.

"Ohhhhh, as absurd as that sounds, it's happening!" replies Grandpa Lynn with gusto, and then he begins to chuckle.

Justin, Grace, Becky, and Wayne look at one another and laugh along with Grandpa at the, yes-indeed, impromptu, amazing, and exciting reunion that is right around the corner.

The big, exciting—and yes—nervous-feeling day of departure arrives. It's a warm mid-September weekend morning in Lake Luzerne. The three adults, two children, four beavers, and four newts pack into Justin's personal four-door pickup and drive to the big grassy field where Linda, the great horned owl, was released. As they are waiting for Pete and the six-passenger helicopter, they put small yellow ear plugs in the beaver's ears.

Huh, thinks Wayne. *They are surprisingly okay with this invasive ear procedure and appear not to be all that nervous.*

Grandpa, who is watching, looks at Wayne and says, "The beavers have a very strong constitution and a great… calming outlook on life. And they trust and love us as we do them."

Wayne replies to his grandpa, "I feel it too, and they calm me down…" and Wayne, knowing that he indeed is nervous about his first helicopter flight, adds, "… a little."

Grandpa Lynn winks at his grandson. He can tell the kids are nervous about their first helicopter flight. And then, they all hear it. Off in the distance, the *wup, wup, wup* of the rotor blades slicing through the air comes to their ears. In under a minute, Pete, the pilot, floats the big yellow and turquoise bird above them and slowly lands. Now, with the otherworldly sights and sounds upon them, the beavers eyes do get big, and they hold on tight to their human friends.

Everyone ducks, walks quickly, boards, and listens carefully to Pete's instructions. They buckle in, don their headphones, and off they go! Becky does not think it is possible, but the beaver's eyes get even bigger as they leave the ground. She has the sedative with her; albeit, they are sniffing away and snuggling with their human friends, doing much better than she expected.

Thirty-five minutes later of total sight-seeing amazement for the kids, beavers, and newts, the helicopter slows down and floats sixty feet above a flat grassy clearing by the Feldspar Brook, with the 5,344-foot-tall Mount Marcy as their backdrop. Fred and Edie's home is a five-minute walk up the hill, and the dammed-up pond with the beaver lodges is across the brook. The two beaver kits sitting with the kids are on one side, and Marty-Bull and Bernadette are on the other side with Justin and Grace. Marty-Bull sees the lodge he grew up in and is flooded with old memories. He tries, but senses nothing from his parents or siblings.

"Wow and hmmm, I hope Mom and Dad are still there," he whispers to himself as the helicopter starts to drop. Closer to the lake, up the hill in a tall pine tree, is a large nest full of neatly stacked twigs and branches where two large eagles roost. Bernice, alarmed and taken by surprise, asks, "Hugh, what is that... thing?!" Hugh looks at his wife and then focuses on the slowly descending noisy...thing. He blinks his eyes, focuses, feels out, and says, "*Ohhh, ohhh,* it's Fred and Edie... and Marty-Bull!... and everyone! They have come home, Bernice! They have all come home!"

Bernice carefully watches the thing as it gets closer to earth and excitedly says, "Hugh, it's Lynn. Hugh, it's Lynn. Minnie and Donald's son is here!"

Hugh looks at Bernice, astonished, and then focuses on the big yellow and turquoise thing going *wup, wup, wup.* "Yes, yes, I feel him too. *Ohhh,* it has been such a long time!"

Bernadette has her eyes closed and is holding onto Grace's arm tightly. The other three beavers are being tightly snuggled by their humans. The helicopter touches down, and as the rotor rpms slow and the noise subsides, she opens her eyes, looks out the window, sees the ground, and says, *"Ohhh,* that was much softer than I expected…ha-ha!"

Into their headphones, they hear Pete the pilot say, "Okay guys and gals, open the doors, duck your heads until you are twenty feet past the rotor, have fun, and I will see you back here in three days at 2 p.m. sharp!"

Becky and Wayne are excited to have Monday and Tuesday off, and so are Justin and Grace. Grandpa Lynn is thinking, *I hope my air mattress pump works.*

Everyone carefully departs and waves goodbye to Pete. He waves goodbye in return as the helicopter ascends into the sky, veers left over the treetops, and is gone. Justin puts a very happy and excited Marty-Bull down and removes his ear plugs. The three remaining beavers are also very happy to feel the ground beneath their webbed feet.

Marty-Bull, happily sniffing the air, stands on his hind feet, pats Bernadette on the shoulder, points at the beaver pond across the way, and yip-yips loudly. Within five seconds, the questioning yip-yips come back, and Marty-Bull excitedly responds. At the edge of the dam, two heads pop up, start uncontrollably yipping, run down the hill, swim across the Feldspar Brook, and Lloyd and Carol hug their oldest son, whom they have not seen in years and never thought possible they would ever see again... but here he is. Over Marty-Bull's shoulder, Carol sees

Grandpa Lynn, the son of their very first Salamander King and Queen, and now she knows how *her* eldest son has come home.

Lloyd says, "Ha! I was wondering what that loud thing in the sky was! *Ohhh,* son… I must go and tell the clan!"

Marty-Bull replies, "And I will help you!" as they swim across the brook, run up the hill, dive into the pond, and start whooping their tails hard with joy. Almost immediately, like smoke signals shared by the Northern Iroquois Nation, whop-whop splashes are heard in return.

On the other side of the brook, Carol hugs Bernadette, who introduces Bruce and Franny to their grandma, and both kits join in the hug.

From the far reaches of the pond, the beavers are coming. They are all coming! The humans chuckle as Wayne says, "Wow! That is a lot of beavers!"

A large group of noisy, happy beavers, eagles, and other wooded creatures have assembled on the shore of Feldspar Brook opposite the beaver dam to welcome Marty-Bull and his family. Grace looks at Justin, and he knowingly nods his head because this assembly happened the first time they were there too.

"I wonder if Rohan and Loki will come visit?" asks Grace.

"That would be very special," replies Justin.

Grandpa Lynn, after hellos and hugs, says, "Hugh, Bernice, and I are going for a walk."

The group of beavers and humans, all chatting and listening to each other's stories, say short goodbyes. Wayne thinks to himself, *He has known Hugh and Bernice since he was a very small boy.*

Grandpa and the eagles head up the hill to Fred and Edie's home and stop a few feet short of their small doorway located in the leaf litter. Grandpa understands that him standing on top of their home might collapse the intricate rooms and hallways. He sits with the eagles, both right in front of him.

After some reminiscing of days long ago, Hugh cannot help noticing, and says, "So, that is the eagle dancer pendant Becky told us about. Have you ever seen the dance performed?"

Lynn replies, "I purchased this Edward Beyuka hand-made pendant at a Drums Along the Hudson pow-wow. And, yes, I have seen the dance performed—actually was taught the dance at another festival, the Native Nation's pow-wow—and joined the Thunderbird Dancers in a ceremonial event. The combination of learning, participating, and having a great time has always turned into some of my favorite experiences. Their interactive pow-wow offered drumming and singing, storytelling, intertribal teaching, and, of course, dancing, of which the eagle dance is very important. I was young then; I am not sure that today my legs are up to the task." The eagles nod their heads, understanding that time can and does reduce physical dexterity, especially among humans.

And then Lynn looks at his two old friends slyly. Earlier in the day, at home in Lake Luzerne, before the helicopter ride, he put the Beyuka eagle dancer pendant and the hand-made Indian print vest on for one reason and one reason only.

He stands up, raises his arms in the air, and recreates the eagle dance for them, chanting the song he was taught by his Native American instructor. Surprised but not surprised, they immediately feel the energy, get excited, and start dancing with him.

Grandpa, now electrified with emotion after seeing the eagles dancing with him, takes the moment very seriously, and he puts his heart, body, and voice into its authenticity. Wayne, Becky, Grace, and Justin, who are with the newts and beavers fifty feet away, hear the song and then see where it comes from.

"Oh my gosh. Grandpa is dancing and singing with the eagles! This is a magical moment," Becky gushes as she remembers when she first met Grandpa Lynn and he told her all about the eagle dancer pendant and the age-old American Indian tradition. She immediately holds her Odd Fellows Rebekah pendant that Grandpa gave her, that she never removes from around her neck, and thinks about what the pendant has represented for years: working together to complete noble goals; the never-failing value of regularity and precision in all my worthy undertakings; peace, love, and charity to bring happiness to others; and purity of character, of thought, of word, and of action. Becky looks at the pendant, loves the symbols and what they stand for…

The Beehive, a representation of cooperative industry teaching the advantages of united efforts in all the noble ministries of the Order.

The Moon and Seven Stars represents the never failing order which pervades the universe of God and all of nature, and suggest to the members the value of system, regularity and precision in all worthy undertakings.

The Dove, a universally recognized emblem of peace, has this significance in the Rebekah Degree. Through the mission of love and charity, of tolerance and forbearance, Rebekah's are to strive to bring happiness to others and to promote "Peace on earth and good will to men."

The Lily, regarded for untold ages as the emblem of purity, is a fitting symbol of the purity of character, of thought, of word, and of action which should always be found and manifested in the heart and life of members of the Rebekah Lodge.

Grace looks up the hill at Grandpa and then at Becky. Taking in the raw emotion on Becky's face, she gets emotional too. Finding and holding onto Justin's hand tightly, she starts to tear up with happiness watching her wonderful and amazing dad being her wonderful and amazing dad.

"He is magical," Grace says to Becky as she holds out her other hand, and Becky takes it.

Justin says to Grace, "Wow, how young he looks."

Grace replies with an emotional "*Awwww.*"

Wayne adds, "Grandpa always says to me, 'you are as young as you feel.'"

Up the hill, Lynn can feel the eyes on the back of his head, freezes his dance steps, and says, "Come, come join us!"

And they all do. Smiling newts are on shoulders, holding onto hair. The joyful beavers make a revolving dance circle of their own around the dancing humans and eagles. What is immediately evident is that everyone is very happy while at the same time taking the dance seriously. This is not a *ha-ha, let's jump around moment.*" This is a dance to honor Hugh and Bernice, their loving protectors and watchers in the sky. This is a moving prayer, thanking God for them, knowing that the grand eagles are in some way a link between Heaven and earth.

The beaver clan looks at one another, steps in, and joins the dance, walking on their hind legs and making eagle wings out of their arms.

Wayne looks at Becky, remembering his time unconscious, stuck beneath the tree underwater, and if it were not for Hugh's piercing shrill call and the fast-acting beavers, Lloyd and Carol, he might not be dancing with them right now.

The deeply reverent and emotional look on Wayne's face is not lost on anyone. Wayne stops dancing, takes a couple steps back, holds his arms out as if they were wings, and bows his head to the eagles and then to Lloyd, Carol, and all the beavers. They all understand, stop dancing, bow back to their Salamander King and friend, and then everyone re-enters the dance. Fred looks at Grandpa Lynn with a knowing appreciation for his grandson Wayne, and Lynn winks back. After another minute, Grandpa Lynn stops, does an ending chant, and everyone sits, laughing and talking.

"Thank you! That was really fun," Bernice expounds.

After reminiscing into the sunset, the humans set up their campsite and make dinner before preparing for bed. And yes, Grandpa's battery-powered air mattress pump worked perfectly. Marty-Bull and his family spend the night in his parents' lodge. Newton and Janine help tidy up Fred and Edie's old vernal pool home and line it with fresh, moist moss. Everyone gets a good night's sleep.

After two more days of the beaver kits playing with their cousins in the pond, and with fond memories shared by all, a surprise guest standing just behind the tree line stops and looks.

Grandpa Lynn turns his head in that direction and softly says to Grace, who is sitting next to him, "Wow, that is a very large buck."

Grace gasps and softly replies, "That is Rohan the Red and his herd! I'm so glad he showed up. This is the icing on the cake, Dad. Unfortunately, there are no candles because Loki and Iostha, the timber wolves, are not with them."

"*Ahhh...* a wolf pack in New York, and Justin never told his command. Good for him."

After Rohan says his hellos, Justin asks him, "Is Loki and his wolf pack still in the area?"

Rohan replies, "Oh yes. His pack is still the only one we have encountered. Their territory right now is around one hundred square miles, so they make it to our area every sixty days or so. I will tell him you said hello. One of the reasons I am here is because he wanted to thank you and your mate for keeping your word to not alert anyone to his presence."

"He is very welcome," Justin replies.

"And give my regards to Iostha," Grace adds.

Rohan nods his head respectfully. "It will be done. Nice to see you again."

Grace cannot help but be in awe of the magnificent stag and his equally magnificent rack of antlers. When he had nodded his head towards her she thought, *all those sharp antler points definitely caught my attention as they must have caught Loki and the wolves attention as well.*

After he checks in with Fred and Edie, the beavers, and the eagles, they all watch the majestic Rohan turn, pick up speed, and—with two thirty-foot leaps—disappear into the woods, his herd right on his tail.

Ugh, it is that dreaded time to say goodbye. Pete and the helicopter are due in the next few minutes, thinks Wayne, looking at all the emotional faces.

When all the hugs are over, Grandpa Lynn states, "We now say goodbye to you, but that is only temporary. Winter is coming, and so is spring. We will be back soon after the snow melts, and that is my promise."

Edie looks at Janine, and, not wanting to jinx anything by talking, she thinks, *Hmmm, and spring time is when the egg balls are laid..."*

The *wup, wup, wup* of the rotor blades is heard in the distance. The kids gently insert new yellow ear plugs into the four beavers' ears for the thirty-five-minute flight back to Linda's field outside Lake Luzerne. The gear is stowed, then they board and buckle up. As the helicopter hovers sixty feet in the sky, the Lake Tear of the Clouds beavers, newts, and eagles all wave their fond good-byes.

Chapter Two

"All Right!"

Some of them have school and work days behind them, while others have taken the day off. It is a beautiful, balmy Saturday, a classic September Indian summer in the mountain-lake-town kind of morning, and the Whitmore's and Bao's are *up and at em'* preparing for the multi-family BBQ that starts at noon. Tom and Justin are setting up the BBQ site with two big grilles for the hot dogs, hamburgers, and veggies. Justin brought his because there are going to be a lot of hungry people—thirty-one, in fact!

Helen and Grace are assembling platters, plates, napkins, glasses, and utensils, all supplied by Nan's parents from their award-winning restaurant. The group made the joint decision based on not wanting to waste paper plates and napkins, which is bad for the environment. Restaurant Manager Chelsey is once again in charge of the small crew helping to set up.

Wayne, Becky, Butch, and Danny are in charge of mowing the lawn, setting up the borrowed picnic tables, benches, and chairs, and... the soccer field and volleyball court! Butch has cruised over on his dad's riding mower to speed up the process. *This is going to be a big, fun social event,* he happily thinks.

Twenty-one adults, including the Whitmore's, Bao's, Hage's, Frasier's, Rector's, Stearns', Barone's, and Carswell's, plus Police Chief Nan Rector's mom and dad; Joel and Christie, who own the Diamond Point Lodge Restaurant on Lake George; Justin's mom and dad; Tue and Margaret; and last but certainly not least, Grandpa Whitmore.

The ten kids include Wayne Whitmore, Becky Hage, Butch and Danny Frasier, Samantha and Eddie Barone, Tim Carswell, Todd Stearns, and Michael Franco, Sergeant Larry Franco's son, who is best friends with Nan's son Evan Rector. Michael and Evan have not seen each other in a while, and because Larry is in charge of the police department today, it made sense to bring Michael with them.

It was explained to everyone prior that cell phones are going to be left in a bedroom and only checked for five minutes after lunch for *emergencies only* because this is a day of conversation, food preparation, eating, clean-up, and then two big sporting events. Police Chief Nan is the only one allowed to carry her cell phone, and she has it on vibration only. At the same time, she feels very confident that Sergeant Franco and his team can handle anything that comes up.

When the Rector family arrives at the BBQ, everyone there has not seen Adrian or Evan in almost two years, so they all want to get a family photo. The Rector family, ecstatically happy to all be together once again, lovingly oblige.

Nan's husband, Adrian, a recently retired Air Force Colonel, is home with their thirteen-year-old son Evan, much to the elation of Nan. Adrian was assigned to Spangdahlem Air Base, which has 5,560 active duty members. The base is located in the federal state of Rheinland-Pfalz in the southwest section of Germany, along the borders of Belgium, Luxembourg, and France. His duties as a Colonel of the 52nd Fighter Wing were to command the strategic mobility mission that provides logistics support for all aircraft, crew, passengers, and cargo for medical operations throughout Europe, Africa, and Southwest Asia. Adrian helped adults and children who needed medical attention, and it wasn't just the military.

Evan attended the Eifel Community School, which is part of the Department of Defense Education system in Europe and operates the schools on the air base with classes ranging from kindergarten through 12th grade. Nan and Adrian made the decision that Evan would go with him because it would broaden his knowledge of the world, and Nan did have a very busy life as the new Police Chief in town. Albeit, even with their almost daily video chats, she missed her husband and son terribly, and now they are home.

The eight picnic tables have been set up in the shape of a big C so food can be brought and taken away through the opening. Plus, everyone can see each other. It does not go unnoticed that Butch Frasier and Samantha Barone are sitting together, and it appears that puppy love is definitely in the air.

Tom Whitmore thinks about the BBQ discussions he started after Wayne and Becky were rescued by Todd Stearns and Eddie Barone, and they have actually come to fruition. Tom replays the moment in his mind. *It was just a couple weeks ago when I said, "I think we..." and he opened his arms to everyone in Chief Nan's conference room, "...should have a family-style backyard BBQ with the Frasier's and invite the Stearns' and the Barone's.*

"Great idea, Tom! You can count on some Hage Lebanese hors d'oeuvres," says Minya, who glances over at Jim as he gives her a nod and a wink.

Nan Rector says, "*Ohhhh,* my mom and dad love a good BBQ. They will put something together that's real Cajun—chicken and sausage jambalaya or crab and shrimp étouffeé."

Justin looks at Grace and says, "Wow!" and then looks from Minya to Tom and says, "This is a great idea! Really bring the community together. And... my mom is famous for her Madame Vo Vietnamese dry-rubbed and marinated BBQ pork with fish sauce, lemongrass, and plenty of garlic." He tilts his head and looks at Grace as if to say, *What do you think?*

Grace laughs heartily. "Wow as well! That... with Diamond Point Lodge Cajun and Hage hors d'oeuvres! Oh, yeah! I'll bring the bibs."

I remember after the school assembly, when Grandpa Lynn, Justin Bao, Jim Hage, and I were chatting with the proud Stearns and Barone parents about the backyard BBQ, thinks Tom.

Terry Stearns says, "Angie makes the best potato salad."

Justin replies, "And that goes great with BBQ. Please, Angie."

Eddie Barone, Sr. looks at his wife Val and says, "You make a great Caesar salad, hon."

"Anchovies on the side?" asks Jim Hage.

"*Ohhh*, definitely makes the Caesar," replies Val, smiling at the wonderful new Vet in town who loves her dog, Tyra, almost as much as she does.

"This is going to be fun!" adds Angie Stearns, who looks at her husband Terry, and says, "BBQ at the Whitmore's!" Both were happily thinking, *Who would have guessed?*

And here that day is!

After everyone has taken a seat, Grandpa Lynn stands and looks at the faces looking back at him, saying, "Hold hands, please. Bless us, O Lord, and for these thy gifts, which we are about to receive through thy bounty for this amazing feast, our wonderful friends, and for our homes and yards where fond memories like this one will linger, we give our thanks. Amen."

"Amen," everyone responds as they unclasp their hands and start passing dishes.

Christy Rector says to the group, "Don't be shy. There is plenty more." Christy catches her daughter Nan's eye and sees how unbelievably happy she is to have her husband and son home. She blows her a kiss, which Nan catches and throws right back—something she has done with her mom since she was a very little girl.

An hour or so later, the really fun and delicious BBQ is over and cleaned up. Chelsey's restaurant crew has loaded the van with plastic totes full of dishes, glasses, and silverware and are on their way back to the Lodge. The picnic tables have been removed from the lawn, and now it is time for the first sporting event of the double-header—the kids' soccer game.

Nan and Adrian's son, Evan, has been away in Europe for almost two years. No one there except his mom and dad knows something that the others don't.

Team captains are Butch and Eddie. Butch picks Samantha as his first pick, of course, and Eddie picks his football teammate, Tim. Butch then picks Danny, Wayne, and Mike. Eddie picks Becky, Todd, and Evan.

Evan is the last pick simply because no one has really played any sports with him. Evan has always attended private schools. The two opposing goalies are Becky and Wayne.

Grandpa has downloaded and studied the rules of soccer, and he is the referee. Grandpa Lynn even has a whistle.

In the huddle, Eddie asks Evan, "Do you know how to play soccer?"

Evan calmly responds, "Yeah, I was on my soccer team at Eifel."

After the coin toss, Grandpa blows the whistle, and as Eddie is running downfield with the ball, his older sister Samantha does a perfect slide tackle, kicking the ball to Butch.

Eddie, not expecting the cool, aggressive move from his sister, laughs. "Boom, Sis! Nice move!"

Butch runs downfield, kicks the ball at a leaping Wayne, which looks to be a certain corner net score. However, before the ball gets to the net, Evan leaps into the air, chest blocks the ball, and deftly runs it through everyone on the field. Then, fifteen feet away from Becky, who is guarding the goal, he has a clear shot and passes the ball to Todd, who has never really played soccer before. Todd gives it his best kick. Becky leaps up, grabs it, and kicks the ball back downfield to the excited hoots and hollers of the parents on the sideline.

Minya Hage, sitting next to Chief Nan, says, "Hmm, I am guessing that was an easy score for Evan, and instead he passed it to Todd."

Nan smiles back at her friend and says, "Evan was the varsity center forward and his team's leading point scorer for the last two seasons. Adrian waited for the soccer season to be over to come home. It was that important; not only to Evan and him but to the team. Germany's number one pro soccer team, Bayern Munich, two-time World Cup champions, told Adrian that they wanted to talk to Evan about their club league to develop his talent further. We all discussed it and agreed. Adrian told their scout he was thirteen years old and to come back when he was seventeen if they and Evan were still interested. Getting an education was more important to Evan. I did some research, and there are actually a few sixteen-year-old professional soccer players that came up from the club leagues."

Minya says, "Wow, Nan. Brilliant, talented, and kind. Fruit didn't fall very far from the tree."

Nan wraps her arm around Minya's shoulder and gives her a loving squeeze. "I'm so happy to have them home," Nan gushes.

The friendly, fun soccer match is over, and the score is tied one-to-one on goals by Todd and Mike. All the kids have a new appreciation for Evan Rector, whom they could not get the ball away from, right foot or left, and who never once took a shot at the goal.

After the soccer match and some hydration, the kids pull up chairs and sit with the remaining adults on the sidelines of the volleyball court to watch their parents in action.

Butch says, "We have a soccer team here, Evan. Are you going to try out?"

Evan smiles back and says, "My Eifel coach and the Lake Luzerne coach have already spoken. I am the new varsity center forward."

"All right!" Butch replies exuberantly as they tap knuckles.

A few chairs away, Wayne says to Becky and Danny, "This is going to be interesting. I have never seen my mom or dad do any kind of sport besides swimming in the lake."

Walking the sixty-foot-long by thirty-foot-wide court to get a closer look, Tue and Margaret Bao are the *imaginary* line judges for the volleyball game. Bright orange tape has been secured to the ground on the four corners of the court, but that's it. After watching the *fun* soccer match, Margaret says to Tue, "I don't think we need to worry about the importance of the lines and any disputes." Tue nods his head in agreement as the players take the court.

Five women are playing against five men, and everyone knows that back in the day, Grace Bao, Nan Rector, and Angie Stearns were on the Lake Luzerne championship-winning volleyball team. Helen Whitmore and Dawn Frasier, who were cheerleaders for Lake Luzerne Eagles football, are on the team and are also no slouches when it comes to v-ball.

The guys' team is made up of their husbands: Tom Whitmore, Justin Bao, Mike Frasier, Terry Stearns, and Adrian Rector, all athletes in their own right—Justin being a former championship-winning track and basketball star.

Before the first ball is served, Grace, Nan, and Angie pop their picnic shirts and shorts off and fling them off the court. Underneath are their still-fitting Lake Luzerne volleyball team uniforms, and as they pull up their knee pads and do high fives, the smack-talking starts!

"Bring it!" Nan says while looking at her completely surprised husband, Adrian.

"Better do some stretches and get warmed up!" resounds Angie, smirking at the unsuspecting Terry, who now has his mouth open.

Grace sticks her tongue out at Justin, who immediately laughs and says, "Wow! Whatever happened to let's have a friendly game of volleyball?!"

The kids on the sidelines completely crack up at their moms' behavior.

Margaret and Tue now take a much closer look at the volleyball court's *imaginary* lines. Margaret tosses the quarter up in the air. Grace yells out, "Heads!" and it lands heads up. Grace says, "You can have first come-first serve. You little boys are going to need every advantage you can get!"

"Ha!" Tom Whitmore, the older brother, replies.

The five *little boys* immediately go into a huddle to plan out their court strategy.

Over at the pond, a small bunny that is madly hop-hopping and zig-zagging through the woods leaps into the pond with a *kersplash* and starts swimming.

Sandy the snapping turtle, sunning on her log nearby, watches the bunny jump into the pond. Sandy shakes her head, thinking to herself, *What odd behavior!* The bunny swims out straight towards the center of the pond, where the water is deep. After 'bunny paddling' for twenty feet or so, the young cottontail is in distress and starts to sink below the surface.

"Uh-oh," Sandy says as she plops off her log into the water. Sandy swims underneath the bunny, rises, and brings her to the surface. The bunny, now riding on top of what she doesn't know, shakes the water from her fur and is grateful for whatever just happened. Sandy slowly turns, taking her back to shore where she will be safe and sound, and that is when she feels the bunny fidgeting around.

Big Ben the snapping turtle, Sandy's boyfriend, still on the log, watches everything that is going on as Sandy comes back to shore and notices a certain someone in the shadows waiting for the bunny's arrival. As Ben silently slips into the pond, he now knows why the bunny went swimming in the first place.

After a few powerful paddles of his four webbed feet Ben catches up with and communicates with Sandy, telling her, "You need to slow down. We have an issue here."

Still a good ways off shore Sandy does, and she immediately feels the bunny stop fidgeting on her shell and also senses that the bunny is now less stressed out.

Ben tells Sandy, "There is a cat waiting in the shadows."

Sandy nods her head, and now they are all on the same page. From just under the surface, Ben sees the cat. The cat, focused on the bunny, is wondering, *Now how is she magically returning to shore and not swimming?*

The cat scrootches down ready to pounce the second the bunny jumps back on dry land. *You are not getting away from me this time my little pretty!*

Paddling six feet from shore Ben stays hidden underwater until he feels his shell break the surface.

All of a sudden, Ben bursts ashore and runs at the cat, hissing loudly! The cat, scared silly, jumps straight up five feet into the air, lands, and sprints away. After twenty or so feet into the woods, the cat stops and looks back, trying to spot the easy prey, and is immediately bombarded by a loudly squawking Grubbins! This time the cat takes off, running hard. Grubbins, still loudly squawking, chases it for a couple hundred feet, right up the back deck steps and through the doggy door into the kitchen! Obviously, this is the cat's home. Grubbins turns and flies back to the pond, chuckling to himself.

Once on shore with the baby bunny, who is still afraid and huddled next to Sandy, the turtles and Grubbins look at each other.

Sandy says, "I do not want to just abandon her. Who knows what else is out there waiting for her to cross their path?"

"I could follow her. Maybe she knows where her home is?" says a thoughtful Grubbins.

And then…her big dad, Jack, hops out of the tree line. He is not mad; he is concerned, glad he found her, and says, "Thank you for your kindness" to Sandy, Ben, and Grubbins. To his daughter he says, "I hope you just learned a big lesson here. I can protect you from the cat, Penny, with my powerful hind feet and claws, but for me to do that, you need to get behind me and not run off alone where the cat can chase you. Until you get much bigger, you need to stay close to the den with your other brothers and sisters."

Penny nods her head. "I was really scared, and I did learn my lesson, Dad."

Her dad exhales and says, "Okay." He then says to the group, "You turn your head away for two seconds, and they are gone."

Bernadette the beaver, who has come to shore to see what the ruckus is about, responds with, "*Ohhh,* you got that right!"

A likewise curious Bruce and Franny, who are just coming ashore and overhearing the conversation, look at each other and chuckle, understanding that they were quite the handful when younger. Across the pond, Marty-Bull is chopping down a sapling. He lovingly looks at his family, thinks about his extended family in Lake Tear of the Clouds, and hopes to see them again.

Penny says, "Thank you all." Jack and Penny hop off, with Penny never leaving her dad's side, hop for hop.

The warm sun is still shining, so Sandy and Ben go back to their log, the beavers go about their chores, and the pond is once again back to normal.

Back at the volleyball game, Adrian serves, Angie double-arm bumps it back over the net, and Tom spikes the ball hard! Grace jumps up and stuffs her older brother Tom's spike!

"Wow's and holy-moly's!" erupt on the sidelines. The girls get the ball back and score off a spike by Nan to more "Wow's, go girl's! and nice!" from the sidelines.

Playing to see who the first team is to get eleven points with a two-point margin, the girls beat the boys eleven to six. After the two teams shake hands, Tom tells his little sister Grace, "You know, I came to all your games. You are just as formidable now as you were then."

Grace looks at her older brother and says, "Aww, thanks, bro," and hugs him.

With the soccer goal nets and the volleyball net stowed away in the Whitmore's' garage, everyone departs back to their lives, happy and satisfied with the day's events and wow, what a great BBQ!

Still just mid-afternoon, Wayne and Becky hop on their bikes to go check on the pond. Todd goes back to his bicycle shop for an awaiting road race bike tune-up, and his dad has a Rochester four-barrel carburetor to rebuild on a 1964 Corvette. Eddie and Tim have a neighborhood YMCA flag football game that all the kids have been invited to play in, including Samantha.

Police Chief Nan, not hearing one word all day from Sergeant Franco, decides not to call him. She thinks to herself, *Larry is more than capable of handling whatever it is, and I am going to let him,* as she looks adoringly at her husband and son, who have all planned to go to Lake George and do some fishing. Doc and Minya Hage are going to go check on the clinic to see who needs help with whom. *Harry, the pot-bellied pig is coming in for a check-up and he's always a handful,* thinks Doc. For some of the other parents, it's Saturday, and there are a lot of to-do lists and yard maintenance chores that need to be addressed.

Tom and Helen Whitmore are sitting in their living room, very satisfied, winding down with Heather, their Scottish Terrier, and Emma, their Calico Cat, snuggled on their laps. Helen says, "Well, that was a huge success, my dear."

Tom looks over at his wife with a grin on his face and says, "We should do this every summer. Especially after me and the boys join the men's winter indoor volleyball league. Next time, we will be ready for you gals."

Helen looks back at her cute husband and says, "Good idea! You go and join the league; it will be good wintertime exercise!" And then, after a short pause, she adds, "We will still kick your butts."

Tom looks back at his wife, cracks a smile, and doesn't say anything because he knows she is probably right. Helen returns his look with a wink and then a sassy laugh that infectiously makes Tom laugh right along with his best friend.

Chapter Three

"Ohhh, I See It."

Early Sunday morning at the pond, His M. watches from the lily pads as a couple of humans, that he figures are around the same age as Justin and Grace, put *something* into the pond. He swims closer to listen in on them talking.

"Goodbye, Buddy. We can't take you with us, and we can't give you to someone else because you are illegal to own. There should be plenty for you to eat here," the man says.

The female nervously asks, "He is going to be rescued, right? You said he will be rescued if we put him here."

"Yes, Buddy will be rescued, I promise. Now, let's get out of here before anyone sees us. This area is posted."

His M. cannot tell what or who the now partially submerged "Buddy" is, so he swims closer. He slowly approaches when, all of a sudden, "Buddy" lunges at him, showing him a whole mouthful of teeth. His M. dives underwater and masterfully twists and turns around the submerged tree branches, but Buddy is right on him, inches away, through the lily pad stems, under the turtle's sunning log, right until the big, powerful bullfrog leaps out of the water at Newton's end of the pond, where he lands in the old vernal pool with a loud thud. Newton and Janine pop out of their emergency escape door and see a very scared bullfrog, which is something Newton has never seen before.

"His M., what is wrong?" he asks.

His M. cannot even answer. He is beside himself, so Newton goes over and wraps his arms around him, and his M. is...shivering?! Newton looks at Janine and says, "You might want to go into our safe room until I find out what's going on."

Janine replies, "No, I am staying right here with you, Newton. We are going to figure this out together." Janine comes over to His M. and hugs him as well. Newton looks at his mate with love and admiration and then focuses back on His Magistrate, the notoriously bold and brash pond manager.

After a while, His M. calms down and says, "We have a problem, Newton. A big, quick-moving problem with a lot of teeth."

"And this problem is in our pond?" asks Newton.

His M. nods his head in affirmation, and then looks out at the pond, scared. "I cannot go in my pond, Newton. I cannot protect my family!"

Newton exhales, scans the pond, and sees nothing, which only creates more mystery and concern. Looking up into the tree, Newton says, "Grubbins, are you there?"

Grubbins immediately pops his head out of his doorway in the tree and lands on a lower branch. He sees both Janine and Newton holding a frightened His M., which is not an occurrence he has ever witnessed before, then lands on the forest floor. He inches close, but does not see any wounds. However, after looking into his eyes, he says, "His M. is in shock." Newton nods his head in the affirmative.

"Can you fly over to Wayne's house and tell him we have an emergency?"

Without hesitation, Grubbins nods his head and takes off.

Walking onto shore, Sandy and Ben, the snapping turtles, come over to see what is going on. They see a distraught His M., and Newton tells them, "Something in the pond with a lot of teeth almost got His M. Grubbins is going to get Wayne."

Big Ben squints his eyes down and says, "Nobody comes into our pond and scares His M." He looks at Sandy and says, "I need to find out who this is."

Sandy blocks his way. "Please, Ben, No, wait for Wayne."

Ben looks at Sandy and says, "This is our pond. I'll be back. Stay here with His M." Brave Ben scurries down and plunges into the pond.

Sandy snuggles down with His M. but can't help looking towards the pond in fear for what might happen to her dear Ben.

Newton goes to the water's edge and watches Ben, who is swimming just below the surface. All of a sudden, he sees a large, strange shape following Ben, and Newton yells, "Ben, it's behind you!" Newton watches as Ben turns and confronts whatever it is, and then the water boils from their interaction.

Sandy is now on the shoreline with Newton and screams, "Ben!" as she dives in and starts swimming towards the commotion to help her beau or die trying.

Halfway there, she sees Ben swimming towards her, who nods towards shore. Once on shore, she sees that a section of Ben's shell has been raked every half inch or so by what she believes are teeth marks. She looks closely at the damage and understands that it is mostly cosmetic. She, herself, has a shell that, when she was a baby turtle, a dog picked her up. A hiss and a couple snaps later, she got dropped, and she still remembers the feel of the tender spots on her shell, which felt just like these look.

Sandy asks, "Are you okay? Did a dog do that to your shell?"

Ben replies, "I'm okay. It was not a dog, but whatever it was, it had my entire shell in its mouth. I bit down on some part of it, and it let me go."

"What exactly did you bite?" asks Newton.

Ben shakes his head and says, "I don't know. It was thick, with tough skin, though. I didn't taste blood, so I didn't penetrate the surface. It let me go and swam away quickly."

That is when His M. chimes in. "It moves very quickly and has a lot of teeth. His name is Buddy; the humans called him Buddy."

Grubbins lands on the low-hanging branch. "Wayne is on his way!"

Just then, they all hear Marty-Bull whopping his tail. Grubbins immediately flies over to the lodge. Marty-Bull is swimming back when Grubbins asks him, "Why were you whopping your tail? What was it?"

Marty-Bull replies, "I do not know what it was, but I scared it away. It was swimming towards the lodge on the surface, and then it just disappeared underwater. I've never smelled anything like it before. If it gets near my lodge again, where Bernadette and the kits are, I will introduce it to my tree choppers!" He bares his huge, razor-sharp front teeth.

Moments later at Newton's home, Wayne and Becky come zooming in on their bicycles. A concerned Sandy asks Becky, "Is Ben okay?"

Becky gets on her knees and touches Ben's shell. "There are no deep puncture wounds, but these are some good gouges that need to be treated. I am going to call my dad."

Ben looks sheepishly at Sandy and says, "Thank you for caring... and you too, Becky…and your dad." Becky looks lovingly at Ben as she rubs the top of his head. "Everything is going to be okay," she says. Sandy looks at Ben and then closes her eyes in relief.

Wayne looks closely at Ben's shell and asks Becky, "What caused those gouges?"

Becky says, "I do not have a clue. Someone with a big mouth and a lot of sharp teeth." Becky grabs her cell phone out of the front pocket of her Osh Kosh B'Gosh overall shorts and dials her dad.

Grubbins says to Wayne, "Marty-Bull chased it away from his lodge over by the swamp and the old fort. He said it was as big as he is, and he has never smelled anything like it before."

His M. softly adds, "The two humans called it Buddy."

Wayne looks at everyone and says, "Please, all of you stay right here. Grubbins, show me where Marty-Bull last saw this thing."

Becky hops to her feet and says, "Dad will be here in thirty minutes. Ben is going to be just fine. You are not going without me."

Wayne smiles at his best friend and says, "Of course. What was I thinking? Let's go!"

Grubbins takes flight, and Wayne and Becky run down the trail, but not at full speed—more like *on-the-lookout* speed. They get to the swamp and see nothing in the pond. Grubbins flies over to the beaver lodge and pokes his head into the air vent. The three beavers holed up in their lodge are on edge. Bernadette tells him, "I am worried about Marty-Bull swimming around outside to protect us." Grubbins says, "He is on his way back home now. Wayne and Becky are here. They will know what to do."

After Marty-Bull arrives back at the lodge Grubbins flies back and says to Wayne and Becky, "I told them as soon as we knew, they would know. Marty-Bull is pretty shaken up, and that's not like him either."

Wayne sits down and says, "Whatever it is, it's out there, and I am guessing it has to breathe. Let's keep our eyes peeled for a head popping through the surface." Wayne thinks for a few seconds and softly surmises, "So... two humans put their... pet, Buddy... in the pond. Where are you, Buddy?" Wayne, thinking ahead about the mysterious pond invader that Grubbins told him about, scans the pond with his binoculars.

Twenty minutes go by as Wayne continues to scan the pond. He watches the placid dark green tree reflected pond turn silver from sun-lit ripples made by the warm breeze and thinks, *Wow, how beautiful!* After giving his eyes a quick break, he continues his slow scan to the right, then to his left, stops, and whispers, "*Ohhh,* I see it. Yep, it has to breathe all right."

Grubbins, who is up in a tree looking at the pond, quietly says, "I see it too."

Becky is straining her eyes on the pond. Wayne points and hands her the binoculars. Becky focuses the setting and says, "Oh, wow! Whoa, you have got to be kidding me!"

Wayne picks up and keys the walkie-talkie. "Wayne to Warden Bao, over."

"Hey, Wayne, what's up?"

"I got an emergency visit from Grubbins, and we are at the pond right now with Becky. Floating forty feet offshore, on the old fort side near the beaver lodge, we are looking at what appears to be a five-to six-foot-long... alligator or maybe a caiman."

Justin gasps. "*Ohhh*... that's just crazy! Somebody dumped their illegal and dangerous pet in Newton's Pond. Hmmm, you know, Nate's from Florida. There are lots of gators in Florida. I will get a hold of him and see if we can come up with a plan." Warden Bao calls Nate. "It appears that someone put their six-foot-long pet alligator, named Buddy, by the way, in our local pond."

"No kidding! I worked on a gator preserve in Punta Gorda. A six-footer should be fairly easy to handle. Can you get the lightweight flat-bottomed rowboat from the barracks?"

"Yup, and that makes perfect sense. Quietly row to it."

"You got it! Okay, I will meet you at the pond in thirty."

At the Fish & Wildlife Barracks, Warden Bao checks in with his Captain, Allen Grammer, to let him know what's going on. Captain

Grammer replies, "This is just ridiculous. We need to find out who this alligator belongs to. Those beaver kits would have been bad enough, but what if a small child was in the pond?"

A few moments after Justin leaves, Captain Grammer reviews the NYS Environmental Conservation Law (Sections 11-0511, 11-0512, 11-035, and 11-0536) that prohibits aspects of possession, transportation, sale, transfer, exchange, importation, and release of wild animals, including alligators, caimans, and crocodiles. In part, aquatic reptiles are regulated in cases where the DEC (Dept. of Environmental Conservation) finds that possession, transportation, importation, or exportation of a species of wildlife or fish would present a danger to the health or welfare of the people of the state or an indigenous fish or wildlife population.

And this is where the Captain has an *ah-ha* moment. Penalties for these offenses include a fine of up to $500 for the first offense and $1,000 for the second offense. Each instance of possession, release, or importation may constitute a separate offense.

"Hmm, possessing and then releasing a six-foot-long alligator is two offenses. Now, how do I find the gator's owners?" Captain Grammer asks himself

Back at Newton's old vernal pool home, Doc Hage has arrived. He looks at the two snapping turtles, who are watching him closely, and says to the one with the obvious fresh gouges on the shell, "Okay, I am going to towel you off and make sure your shell is completely dry. In a minute or so, I will be cleaning these gouged areas with betadine, and then I will apply a strong healing cream."

"His name is Ben, Dad, and that is Sandy," adds Becky, coming back down the trail with Wayne as they wait for Warden Bao to arrive.

Without missing a beat or being surprised, Doc Hage continues with, "Ben, I am using a Q-tip to apply the betadine on the gouge spots so they will not get infected. We will let this dry because we do not want any of it to get into your eyes, ears, or mouth. It can irritate you. Okay, now I am going to apply a healing cream, silver sulfadiazine, which does require a prescription. And Becky here will keep a tube of this in her daypack for one more application later today. This cream is water-soluble and will dissolve quickly, so stay out of the water today, Ben. Can you do that?" Doc Hage looks at the turtle and laughs. "*Annnd...* Ben nods his head to me, just like he understands the question. I should be used to it by now." Doc Hage softly rubs Ben's head, who closes his eyes and welcomes his touch.

Wayne tells Doc Hage, "A five-to six-foot-long alligator did that. Warden Bao is on his way right now. He's stopping at his barracks to pick up a rowboat."

"Good. That critter does not belong in our pond," Doc Hage replies. "Okay, Ben. You should heal very quickly. Bye-bye kids. I have three baby goats coming in for their first checkup. Vaccines, a tetanus shot, and a dewormer. Let me know how the gator-wrangling goes," Then he hops in his SUV, waving goodbye.

Thirty minutes later, Justin arrives at the pond and meets up with Wayne and Becky. He backs the boat trailer in so it is ten feet away from the pond. Nate shows up and grabs one side, Justin holds the other side, and they walk the lightweight rowboat halfway into the pond.

Nate takes his powerful Steiner binoculars and scans the pond where Wayne points. "Holy shi... sh-ka-bab, that's a gator all right! Okay. I haven't been gator-wrangling in years. This is going to be fun! I'm going to the market to get some raw chicken breasts. Be right back." He hops in his truck and takes off.

Becky looks at Justin and says, "This is fun for Nate? I would be scared to death."

Justin replies, "He spent his childhood working on a gator preserve in Florida. If anyone in this area knows how to safely handle gators, it's Nate."

At the Luzerne Market, on his way to the check-out counter, Nate runs into Diane and the big black and white, blue-eyed Malamute left behind by his owners that had gone feral and that he almost shot.

He thinks to himself, *God bless Grace for not only netting and saving the dog but also sending her to school to become a service dog.* Nate has been friends with Diane since grade school. She, as an Army Medic, had multiple traumatic experiences in Afghanistan and acquired PTSD (Post Traumatic Stress Disorder), and this dog basically saved her life.

"Hey, Diane! How are you guys doing?" Nate gets on one knee and pets the big dog, who is wearing a cute orange camo vest that says "Service Dog" on it.

Diane replies with, "Great, actually. Her name is Ella."

Nate rubs the sides of her neck and says, "Why, hello, Ella!" The dog clearly loves having her neck fur rubbed.

"I ran out of Greenies and needed a few other things. Are you having a chicken barbecue, Nate?"

Nate does not want to tell her that the chicken breasts are for an alligator in the pond, so he says, "I am actually picking them up for Justin and Grace."

"*Ohhhh*, say hello to them for me. I think of Grace daily and how wonderful Ella and my life is because of her." She giggles and says, "I am going on a dinner date tonight. First one in a long time!"

Nate gushes, "That is wonderful. He is one very lucky guy!"

Diane smiles, and Nate kisses her cheek, which makes her blush. He looks into her eyes and sees that she is truly happy. "Have fun! Where are you going?" Nate asks.

"Diamond Point Lodge," Diane says with a happy wow look.

"*Niiiiiiice*," Nate replies, knowing what a great and prestigious restaurant Police Chief Nan's parents have established over the years.

"Well, great seeing you,"

Diane gives him a happy toodle-ooh finger wave and they part ways.

Back at the pond, Nate tells Justin, "I ran into Diane and her service dog Ella, that big Malamute Grace rescued with the net cannon. She wanted me to say hi to you guys. She looked great and happy."

"Beautiful. I will tell Grace. She will be very pleased," Justin replies.

"Okay, let's do this," Nate says, now with a note of seriousness in his voice and on his face.

The guys strip down to just a pair of shorts and a life vest. Justin rows, and Nate sits in the bow. Becky thinks to herself, *Whoa, Nate and Justin are two buff dudes.*

Wayne says, "Hoo-hoo, the new workout room at their office is obviously being used."

Becky responds, "Ha, no doubt about that."

Justin rows slowly over to the floating alligator. Nate calls him by name. "Hey Buddy, want some chicken?" The alligator slowly turns towards them. "Yup, Justin, he knows his name," Nate says quietly. As the rowboat gently floats towards the alligator, Nate waves the raw chicken breast half in and half out of the water.

The alligator immediately smells the familiar odor and swims toward him. Nate smiles to himself, remembering his younger days in Florida when he worked with many alligators this size and bigger. "The raw chicken breast gets em' every time, ha-ha," he chuckles.

Nate wiggles the chicken over Buddy's head, who reaches up, gulps it down and is looking for some more. Nate gives him another chicken breast that he gulps down easily. Nate then slips slowly, waist-deep, into the pond and walks over to the floating alligator, much to the shock and surprise of everyone there. "Hey Buddy, how's it going? You liked that chicken, didn't you?" The alligator does not swim away, and Nate gently picks up and cradles the alligator's body with both hands.

Justin, concerned that the alligator may bite Nate or him once in the boat, asks, "Do you want to grab his nose? I've got the electrical tape."

Nate, with a big smile on his face, brings the gator over to the boat and says, "He definitely was someone's pet and is used to being handled. He's…okay. Buddy is cool."

Justin exhales, a little nervous, but trusts his best buddy's instincts. Nate puts Buddy in the boat who just sits there, hops in and Justin rows back to shore.

Justin and Nate pull the front half of the boat onto land. All the pond dwellers, hidden from view, are looking at the alligator go to shore in the boat and are relieved and happy the thing with all the teeth is in the boat and not in the pond. Nate dips his hand in the pond and sprinkles some water on Buddy to keep him moist and calm—and yes, he is very relaxed.

Grace, whom Justin had called on his way to the pond with the rowboat, backs her pickup in, and she has a large empty dog cage in the bed.

As she walks over to the rowboat, Nate goes to pick Buddy up, and Grace says, "You can leave him in the boat, Nate; I'll get him." She turns to Buddy and says, "So, Buddy, we need to get to know one another, seeing how you are going to be in my pet motel until the FedEx shipping box arrives."

Wayne and Becky are watching as Grace gently picks Buddy up, who lets her. The kids look to the pond, and there—with their faces at water level out between the lily pads—are His Magistrate, Marty-Bull, Bernadette, Newton, and Janine, who all nod their heads in appreciation.

Over on their sunning log, with a small army of supportive turtle friends, Sandy and Ben—who are not going in the water as per Dr. Hage's orders—also nod their heads in appreciation.

Nate grabs his cell phone out of his truck and makes a call to the gator preserve in Punta Gorda, Florida, where he worked as a kid and spent many of his summers. "Yup, a six-footer and tame as all get out. Uh-huh, we are going to ship him to you via FedEx Overnight. Okay, thanks, and hey, say hi to everyone."

"Captain Grammer would really like to know who did this," remarks Justin.

Grace replies, "Hmmm, a while back a young couple came into my store to get some medication for mouth rot in their reptile. I asked them what kind of reptile it was, and before they told me, they asked me if I could keep it quiet. You know me. Worried more about the animal than the law, I said yes. So, they told me that they had a very small alligator. For the correct dosage amount I asked them how much they thought it weighed, and they hesitated and then said thirty-five to forty pounds. I knew it wasn't a small alligator. I gave them the per-weight diluted medication and said, "This is a twice-daily topical application of chlorhexidine, a product called Nolvasan. I told them it was important to use the solution gently and to not scrub the spot, which would only irritate the mouth further. I told them to gently dab on hydrogen peroxide with a Q-tip between doses, and it worked. And… they paid by credit card. I will call Captain Grammer with the information on Monday. Is this going to be a reprimand for these folks?"

Justin replies, "A big reprimand and possibly a substantial fine."

Grace shakes her head. "They could have brought the gator to me, and I would have sent it to Florida, just like I am doing now. Oh well."

Justin, Nate, Wayne, and Becky shake their heads, saddened by the pet owner's bad behavior.

Justin says to Wayne and Becky, "Well, another successful pond adventure. From a goldfish to a gator. Who woulda guessed?"

After a kiss goodbye between Grace and Justin, they all hop in their trucks and depart.

Once back at her pet store in Queensbury, Grace places Buddy in the enclosure with the pool where she kept Ben the snapping turtle when he was injured. Sharon, Grace's Pet Store employee and aspiring Vet Tech who is a junior in college, has all the instructions to set up the safe and healthy alligator shipping with FedEx, just like they did with the Tam Dao newts to Vietnam.

As Grace is prepping Buddy's temporary home, Sharon says, "Okay, we should get the FedEx six-by-two-foot wooden ventilated, insulated, and cushioned box tomorrow. They told me not to ship live on Mondays and Thursdays. Mondays are FedEx's busiest days, and extended delays are likely. Shipping on Thursday increases the risk of your shipment getting hung up over the weekend. Tuesdays and Wednesdays remain the safest live shipping days, FedEx-wise. They are also supplying the Lacey Act IATA label, and they will use their plane with the temperature and humidity controlled compartment."

Grace replies, "Great, today is Sunday, so we should be ready for a Tuesday overnight shipment. Good job."

On Monday, Grace calls Captain Grammer and gives him the alligator owner's credit card information and former address. After a short search, he finds that the couple has moved to Massachusetts. "Let's see…New York and Massachusetts both ban any type of ownership of a pet alligator. All right, time to call the local game warden office in Massachusetts."

Wayne and Becky, now sitting under the tree at Newton and Janine's home, are with the two newts, Sandy and Ben, His M., and Grubbins. The beavers are all chopping down and stockpiling saplings for the winter months. Newton is on Wayne's shoulder, and Janine is on Becky's. His M. jumps into Wayne's lap, hugs him, and then Becky's lap.

Becky lovingly pets His M. and after a moment says, "Come here, Ben, so I can apply some more of the silver sulfadiazine healing cream that Dad gave me.

Ben walks over and says, "Thanks, Becky."

Grubbins, who earlier overheard the game wardens talking, says, "So that... alligator, uh, they have a lot of those in Florida, I assume?"

Becky looks at her smart phone, tap, tap, taps, and says, "Wow. One point, three million of them. The average size is seven feet long, but the males can be fourteen feet long!"

Grubbins tilts his head and asks, "What does million mean?"

Wayne says to Becky, "Lie down, Beck," and she does, holding onto Janine on her shoulder and His M. in her lap. Wayne lies down, touches her feet with his, and holds his arm up. "Grubbins, come here." Newton is now on Wayne's head, holding onto his hair.

Grubbins lands on his hand and looks down at the two kids. Janine crawls over Becky to get closer to hear what Wayne is saying.

Wayne continues with, "Becky and I are now approximately eight feet long. Now think about covering the entire town of Lake Luzerne, every yard, every street from here to the falls, with us this size, and you still wouldn't even be close to a million."

Becky says to Grubbins, "And we are just the average size of one alligator in Florida. Many are much larger."

"Wow!" Grubbins responds as Wayne and Becky sit up. Newton moves back down to Wayne's shoulder as Grubbins hops down to the ground.

His M. says in a serious tone, "I bet there are a lot less frogs in Florida."

Ben adds, "And snapping turtles!"

Becky tap-taps her smart phone and replies, "Alligators tend to eat mostly fish, small mammals, birds, and yes, turtles, but frogs aren't mentioned." She does another search and says, "There are twenty-seven frog species in Florida, and they cover the entire state, so with the number of eggs frogs lay, I think they are doing just fine." His M. is relieved and exhales a biiiig exhale.

Newton replies, "Well... I am very happy we are in Lake Luzerne, not Florida, and I believe the one and only alligator that was here is in good hands and will never be seen again, thanks to our wonderful friends."

"Our pleasure. Well, I have yard chores and homework to do, so I will see you guys after school tomorrow," Wayne replies to his animal friends.

To His M., still sitting on her lap and holding onto her finger, Becky says, "Are you okay to go back in the pond?"

His. M. mightily inhales and exhales. "Why of course, dear Becky," he replies as he gives her finger and squeeze and then hop-hops and launches himself into the lily pads where he is greeted by a huge squadron of frogs awaiting his return and want to know if the terror of the pond is gone for good.

After a few minutes in his truck Nate calls Justin. "Hey, buddy. That was great! I wanted to ask you something. My dad lives on Canadarago Lake in Richfield Springs. Every Spring is the annual carp bow fishing derby. You want to go? It's a big fund raiser for the lake and it's a lot of fun. Invite whomever you want. Food for thought."

"Interesting, Nate. Never been bow fishing. I will ask around. Thanks"

Chapter Four

"Where are you?"

After school the next day, Wayne and Becky are knee-deep in the lily pads. They net and examine a frog, a green newt, and a painted turtle and find them all very healthy. Wayne says to Becky, "You know, we should walk the back trail around the reservoir to look for any potential garbage sites. Since Butch, Danny, and their dad took the fort down with Justin, there hasn't been any trash dumped in the pond, but we have never checked the Calamity Creek area. The back road gate to the reservoir is locked, and ATVs are not allowed, but you never know."

"Good idea; let's go check it out," Becky replies.

Newton, who is on Wayne's shoulder, says, "Janine and I are going to find His Magistrate and go for a swim."

Janine, who is on Becky's shoulder, adds, "The pond water is so refreshing. Bye!" as they both dive off their perspective human's shoulders and into the water.

Becky looks at Wayne and smiles, loving their salamander friends and their otherworldly ability to communicate with them.

They walk on land and clean off some pond plant debris, shake, and lean their nets up against their bikes to dry out. A few minutes later, as the reservoir trail gets farther away from the creek and closer to the road and homes, Wayne says, "Not even a cigarette butt or a candy wrapper. This is great!"

Becky stops. "Did you hear that, Wayne?"

Wayne stops and hears a slight rustling and some faint squeaks. They walk towards the sound and see four tiny baby striped skunks, who see them and stop dead in their tracks.

Wayne says, "Uh, oh. If Mom is nearby, she is going to protect her kits, and we could get blasted. If you see her, squint your eyes, hold your breath, and run."

Becky nervously looks around. "Wouldn't she be with them?"

Wayne takes a closer look at the small kits and says, "Hmm, they are tiny—probably not weaned yet. Yeah, Mom should be with them."

He alerts to a dog barking and looks through the trees to a home about one hundred yards away. The bark does not become louder or closer, so the dog is obviously leash secured to something in the yard because there is no fence.

Wayne looks at Becky and sits down, six feet away from the four kits. Becky looks at Wayne, slowly says, "*Ohh-kaaay,*" and keeps standing as she scans the woods for Mom. A moment later, she sits down next to him and says, "Dang. I wish we had Newton with us. He could communicate with them.

Wayne replies, "Well, we can't just leave them here, so let's give it a shot." And then to the four kits, Wayne softly says, "Hi, little ones. Where is your mom?"

The kittens, hearing the soft, welcoming voice, scamper over to the two kids. Becky squints her eyes and asks Wayne, "Can they spray us?"

Wayne smiles and chuckles. "They can, but it's not going to be anything remotely like an adult. At this age, it's actually a minty smell. Baby skunks rarely spray, but that doesn't mean it never happens. Grandpa's neighbor raised some baby skunks, and he showed me what to look out for. There are a couple warning signs: a few shakes of its head and bobbing up and down on its hind legs mean back away."

Becky looks at Wayne and says, "Minty. *Thaaat's*... interesting."

The little seven-week-old skunks waddle within inches of their bare legs, looking up at the two humans. There was no head shaking or body-bobbing, so Wayne reaches down, gently picks two of them up, puts them on his lap, and starts petting them.

Becky, tickled by Wayne's unending knowledge and love of animals—which obviously includes baby skunks—does the same with the other two. Still, on the side of being cautious, after a few seconds, Becky stops holding her breath, inhales and exhales, and says, "*Ahhhh,* okay. So, we have four really adorable baby skunks in our laps. Now what?"

Wayne smiles, reaches down, grabs his walkie-talkie, and says, "Now we call Game Warden, Justin Bao, and... keep on the lookout for Momma Skunk." Becky immediately turns her head in both directions to take a good look.

Back at the pond, Newton, Janine, and His M. are taking a swim. Janine slides through the water and says, "*Ahhhh.*"

"*Ohhh,* this does feel great, Janine, knowing that there is nothing in the pond that is going to eat me," chuckles His M.

They glide over towards the lodge and are met by the four beavers that are all doing the same thing: taking a swim.

"Pride of ownership!," Marty-Bull announces. "And, once again, swimming around freely in our safe home. That creature was something else. I saw Grace load it into her truck and drive off."

Bernadette adds, "Big thanks to our human family!"

Bruce adds, "And… Dad is not working! Let's go chase the turtles!"

His sister Franny chimes in with a chuckle. "Oh, Dad and Mom aren't going to chase the turtles."

Marty-Bull looks at Bernadette, winks, and dives underneath the lily pads, scattering turtles everywhere. They know he's just playing with them. Marty-Bull pops back up to the surface with a big smile on his face. "I found a whole bunch of them! I also did this when I was your age, Bruce. I'm pretty good at it too."

Bernadette and the kits laugh out loud at their funny dad as the turtles settle back into their lily pads waiting to ambush a minnow, smirking at Mary-Bull.

His M., caught up in the moment, says, "Well, Ol' Bull Boy... I bet you can't catch me." He squints down at Marty-Bull, who squints back and kersplashes his tail on the surface as he takes off after His M., who kicks his strong legs and large webbed feet, propelling his body in and out of the lily pad stems. Ol' Marty-Bull is hot on his trail. Newton, Janine, Bernadette, Franny, Bruce, and a whole bunch of frogs and turtles are giddy, watching their workaholic dad and friend actually play with His M.

After a couple minutes, Marty-Bull floats back with His M sitting on his neck, both tuckered out and giggling.

"I came right up underneath you," says Marty-Bull.

"Well, I did stop swimming," His M. replies.

Newton says, "And this, my dear friends, is how it is here in our little pond in the woods," as Janine snuggles right up to him.

Just then, Warden Bao appears on the shoreline and calls out, "Newton, Janine... Hey, where are you guys?"

Moments later, Warden Bao shows up on the access road behind Calamity Creek, and he has Newton on one shoulder and Janine on the other. Becky, seeing the two ancient red efts, smiles and says, "Smart move, Justin."

Justin replies, "Well, I thought if we ran into Momma Skunk, it would be good to have an intermediary with us." He laughs along with Becky and Wayne. Justin takes out his cell phone, calls Judy the rehabber, and says, "Hey Judy. I am here behind the Lake Luzerne Reservoir with Wayne and Becky, who have four tiny baby skunks. Can I bring them to you?"

Judy responds with, "Where are you, exactly?"

Justin, with a quizzical look on his face at her odd question, tells her, "About one hundred yards inside the back gate to the reservoir just off the road. Why do you ask?"

Judy laughs. "Because I am parked at the back gate. Come unlock it."

"Huh, really! Okay, here I come."

Justin hops in his truck, unlocks the gate, and pushes the two aluminum arms to the side. He walks over to Judy and cannot, for the life of him, understand why Judy is standing there, arms crossed, with a huge smile on her face.

Judy walks to the back of her pickup truck, drops the tailgate, and holds out her hand pointing at the door of a cat carrier. Justin looks inside, and there is Momma Skunk!

Judy looks at Justin and says, "Hey, you had one of those big red efts on your shoulder when we let the big great horned owl go. Now you have... two? They are the largest red efts I have ever seen."

"I know. Lake Luzerne has really big red efts. They are my... pets. We, uh, go everywhere together," Justin replies, not knowing exactly what to say. Newton, listening in, gets a big kick out of his smart response and wraps his tail around Justin's neck to let Justin know he is listening. "Where did you find the skunk?"

Judy smiles at Justin and his out of the ordinary two pet red efts and says, "I just picked her up five minutes ago. This couple who live right there"—she points through the trees—"called me and told me they had a skunk in a Havahart trap that they believe sprayed their dog. I took one look at her, saw that she was nursing, put her in the cat carrier, and was going to take her back into the woods to see if I could find the kits."

The entire time, Newton and Janine are looking at the big skunk, who is looking right back at them and nodding her head up and down. Justin sees this and is happy with his decision to get the two ancient red efts for this mission.

Justin smiles at his wonderful, smart, friend Judy and says, "Leave your truck. Hop in. I will take you and Mom here, right to them."

A minute later, Justin parks the truck. Wayne and Becky, riddled with anticipation as to what's happening, are now standing up, holding the kits in their arms.

Judy says, "Umm, I suggest you put the kits on the ground. I have a surprise for them, and you might not want to be holding them when they get surprised." Justin laughs out loud.

The kids set the four baby skunks on the ground as Judy walks towards them with the cat carrier. She sets the carrier down and opens the door. Momma Skunk runs out and goes right to her kits, who are all squeaking loudly. Momma then does something that surprises Judy. She waddles over to Wayne and Becky. Wayne, knowing Newton is there, immediately sits down, and so does Becky. Judy looks at them, wondering what they know that she doesn't. She is ready to run away to not get sprayed but she has to admire the kids for their bravery and obvious trust of the big mom. *And wow! Momma Skunk hops right into Becky's lap, hugs her, and then crawls over and hugs Wayne. Unbelievable!* After a brief moment of hugs and pets, Momma climbs off of Wayne's lap. The kits follow her a few feet into the woods where she lies down, and the kits snuggle in and start nursing. Momma Skunk looks at the humans, and they can all see the love in her eyes. With Newton and Janine's intervention, she knows they all helped reunite her with her kits.

Becky says, "Very cool, that worked out better than expected."

Judy responds with, "Definitely not something you see every day...and look how relaxed they all are. I expected them to be long gone. Huh. It was meant to be."

Becky stands and asks her, "Are you the rehabber that got the big female owl back to her home?"

"Yes, I am. And are you Becky, the daughter of Dr. Jim Hage, who surgically fixed her wing?"

"That would be me," Becky says.

Judy walks over and gives Becky a big hug. As she backs away, she still holds onto Becky at arms' length and says, "You and your dad are the number one reason why she is flying strong and made my job easy."

"She is such a beautiful owl. And my dad is brilliant. Feel free to call him if you get an animal that has been injured," says a very proud Rebecca Hage.

"Thank you, and I look forward to meeting him and your mom. Justin told me that it's a real team effort at the clinic."

"We do have a great team", Becky responds

After a brief pause in the conversation, Justin says to Judy, "I would like to meet the people who trapped a nursing skunk. Care to join me?"

"Absolutely; let's go!" Judy replies.

Justin asks, "You guys want to go with us?"

Wayne and Becky look at each other. Becky cocks her head to one side, which means she can go either way. Wayne tells Justin, "I think we are going to complete our reservoir trail walk, and then go to the clinic to see what's going on there." Becky nods her head in agreement.

"Okay, if you need me, you know how to reach me," as he pats his walkie-talkie attached to his warden's vest.

Justin and Judy walk through the woods and knock on the back door, which opens. Standing there is a forty-something man and woman. "Hi, I am game warden Justin Bao, do you have a minute?" "Ummm, sure." says the husband. "Judy told me that you trapped the skunk and thank you for doing that instead of killing her. But, I need you to understand that these woods are the skunks home and that it isn't right for them to be threatened or removed from their home, where they have lived for generations." The woman replies with, "I agree. Our dog got sprayed and we over reacted. Now we are looking at purchasing an invisible fence for our dog, Cinders, so we don't have to tie him up—and we do have a big yard."

Her husband, who obviously does not care for skunks, finally nods his head in agreement. "Yeah, I guess you are right. Do unto others— even skunks—as you would have them do unto you, right?" he asks.

His wife gives him a quick hug and says, "Right! And good attitude!"

"They are very smart and quite lovable," Judy replies.

Newton tugs on Justin's ear and points. Justin says to Judy, "Newton would like to sit on your shoulder."

Judy looks at Justin and Newton quizzically, and says, "Okay."

Justin puts Newton on her shoulder. Judy kneels and talks to the big black male Labrador Retriever named Cinders, who looks from Judy to Newton and back to Judy, where he sticks his paw out and shakes her hand. As Judy is shaking the dog's hand, she somehow knows that he has learned his lesson and will leave the skunks alone.

Judy gets up and walks back to the owners with Newton still on her shoulder. And for some reason unknown to her, she really feels comfortable having him there. Judy tells the owners, "I saw her extended teets and knew that the skunk was nursing. It is that time of year. During the first six to eight weeks of their lives, baby skunks are completely dependent on their mother, feeding on her milk four to six times a day. They will sleep in the den all day as their mother feeds them and goes out to collect food for herself. They stay in the den until about eight weeks, and then follow the mother to learn foraging. That was more than likely what was happening when Momma Skunk encountered your dog.

I do believe Cinders learned his lesson with the skunk, but there are bears, porcupines, and raccoons in these woods, so getting an invisible fence is still a good idea. There is no digging or wire to bury. Sets up in just a few hours. Creates a wireless, secure barrier around your yard to not only protect the wild animals, but Cinders as well. Cinders will wear a rechargeable, waterproof collar with five adjustable correction levels. Really easy and safe."

Cinder's dad says, "Okay, that sounds like a solid plan. We will go down to O'Donnell's Hardware Store, and if Phil doesn't have one in stock, we will order one." They all shake hands and part ways.

Justin takes Judy back to her truck, where she reluctantly hands over Newton. "This guy is special, Justin. I felt him…thinking or—I don't know… something."

Justin looks back at Judy and smiles, "I know; that is why they go everywhere with me."

They trade hugs and goodbyes. Justin and the two red efts lock the gate, and he heads back down the access road. There, he runs into Becky and Wayne and parks his truck.

Justin says, "I had an encounter with a skunk when I was in Boy Scouts. Would you like to hear about it?"

Wayne and Becky look back and say, "Definitely," and "I'd love to hear about it!"

"I was ten years old and sleeping in a tent near the deepest part of the woods where a stream was just down the embankment at our local Boy Scout camp. It was not even dawn when I was awakened by a strange noise outside the tent. *Errrr, errrr, errrr.* I got up, and whoa—there was a giant skunk with its head stuck inside our large jiffy peanut butter glass jar that we stupidly left outside the tent.

"So, the skunk had its two paws on the rim of the opening, trying to push it off, going *err, err* with every straining push. My tent-mate obviously had not put the lid back on very tight because the skunk un-screwed it! Anyway, I went over and saw the skunk looking right at me through the glass. I stood on the jar, and the very strong skunk pulled the bottle right out from underneath my foot. I actually bent down and tried to pull the jar off with my hands, but that did not work, so I sat down, grabbed the skunk with one hand and the jar with the other, and gently wrenched it off his head. I put the jar down, and now I have this huge wild skunk sitting in my lap. And then... the skunk just sat there, licked its paws, and cleaned its face, looking at me the entire time. After a minute or so, it slowly waddled back into the woods. That was when I learned that animals understand a lot more than we think they do."

Newton adds, "That skunk went back to its family and told them how nice you were."

"And to stay away from any human food," adds Janine. "But who knows who listened to that?"

Wayne adds, "A skunk can smell peanut butter from half a mile away, and it is addictive to them; so yeah, lock the jar up in a tight container."

"Yup," Justin agrees, and, after a brief silence, asks, "You guys want a ride back to your bikes?"

Wayne looks at Becky, who says, "No thanks. We are going to continue our litter search loop around the reservoir and then go to the clinic."

"Okay. Say hi to your mom and dad for me." Justin walks to his truck, talking to the newts on each shoulder.

Wayne and Becky, both watching their friend drive away, look at each other and smile, knowing exactly how wonderful that moment of conversation was.

Chapter Five

"You Can Do It!"

It's the big, nervously awaited Saturday. Eddie and Tim's first football game on the Lake Luzerne JV defensive squad they tried out for and won starter positions on, and they both are nervous as they run onto the field with their team for the first time. There are lots of complex plays in practice to remember and apply to an offensive squad that knows about the two rookies and seriously wants them not to succeed. And neither does the hometown Warrensburg crowd.

It's a brisk, sunny, fall afternoon, and a lot of people are not only wearing coats but hats and gloves as well.

At the end of the 4th quarter, the score is Lake Luzerne Eagles 13, Warrensburg Wolverines 14. The two rookies are sitting together on the bench when Eddie tells Tim, "We've got to stop them now!"

Coach yells, "Okay defense—do your job!"

The high-kicking, pom-pom-twirling cheerleaders and the Warrensburg school's marching band's crisp snare drums and blatting horns cheering on their team come to an abrupt stop as play is about to resume. There are twenty-six seconds left in the game, and the Warrensburg offense is thirty-three yards away from the end zone.

Warrensburg has a good kicker and wants a field goal that will make Lake Luzerne have to get a touchdown to win if any time remains on the clock, which the Warrensburg coaches are trying very hard to use up as well.

It's third down; they just took their second to last time out, and now they need to be ten more yards closer to the goal post for the kick to be accurate on this brisk, windy day. Their kicker is practicing on the sideline.

The ball is snapped, and the clock once again starts ticking down. Carlton, the Wolverines quarterback, fakes a handoff to his fullback and goes back to pass a quick screen to number twelve. Brad, his favorite target, is someone he feels confident will get them the needed yardage. Brad is being tightly double-covered, so he looks to his left for target number two, who is blanketed as well.

Eddie Barone and Tim Carswell, who not only worked really hard in practice but spent weekends studying to get their grades up, have so far played a great game. Eddie, who made the roster because of his speed and uncanny ability to knock the passed ball away before it gets to a receiver, is a linebacker. And Tim, because of his size and unrelenting determination, is a tackle.

What Carlton does not realize is that the captain of the Lake Luzerne Defense called for a red dog blitz. As soon as the ball is snapped, Tim Carswell starts pushing his way through the offensive line, and two seconds later, Eddie Barone flies in right behind him and is now chasing down the quarterback, who sees him and takes off running.

Everyone in the Lake Luzerne bleachers stands and starts yelling at the top of their lungs, "Woooow!" "Yeeees! "Go Eddie! Get the quarterback!"

Carlton's second favorite target, a tall tight end, breaks clear of the Eagles safety and is running towards the end zone. Carlton sees him get open, and so do the Lake Luzerne coaches, who start yelling and pointing.

Carlton goes to pass the football when Eddie leaps in and swats at it.

"FUMBLE!" everyone screams on both sides of the field!

Eddie reaches down but cannot grab the helter-skelter, bouncing football. Carlton, who is also fighting hard to regain possession of the ball, gets his hands around it and scoops it up off the turf. As he stands upright to pass, Eddie rips the ball out of his hands and starts running for Warrensburg's end zone, quickly outdistancing Carlton.

Butch, Samantha, Danny, Wayne, Becky, all the students, and the entire crowd go hysterical! Off duty security for the game, Lake Luzerne police officer Larry Franco, hears and sees the aluminum bleachers creaking up and down under the weight of the jumping up and down crowd, and says to himself, "Whoa!"

Eddie's head coach and two assistant coaches are now running down the sidelines screaming, "Go Eddie, go! He needs blocking! Somebody hit number twelve! Somebody hit number twelve!"

Eddie is running as fast as he can, and so is the entire offensive unit of Warrensburg, chasing him, including their well-known tough speedster, Brad, their star tight end. He is wearing the notorious number twelve jersey that, at the start of today's game, was crisp white, and is now heavily grass-stained.

In the first half, Eddie batted two passes away from Brad, and now it's payback time. Eddie zigs and zags, and so does Brad, who is closing the gap. They run past the fifty-yard line, the forty-yard line, the thirty, and then the twenty. Brad's finger tips are mere inches away from Eddie's back.

Noticed by the local radio station DJ covering the game from the booth above the bleachers, the scoreboard clock continues to tick down. 00:12 seconds, 00:11 seconds... "Ten seconds remain! Can Brad stop him and get a win for Warrensburg?" yells the DJ.

Justin Bao, among many other local residents of Lake Luzerne listening in while driving, turns the volume up a notch and grits his teeth. "Go Eddie, go! You can do it!" he yells to the cab of his pickup truck.

Brad grabs Eddie's jersey, slowing him down, but Eddie continues to twist, move, and fight for every inch. But Brad is not a rookie; he gets an arm around his waist and is wrenching Eddie to the ground. Before Eddie's knee touches the turf, he looks to his right, and there is Timmy Carswell running alongside, who holds out his hands! Eddie laterals the ball to him, and Tim catches it just as Brad and Eddie crash into each other and slide onto the freshly mowed and slightly trampled, verdant gridiron field.

Tim tucks the ball in tight and runs towards the end zone. Two yards away, he is tackled by one, two, and then three Warrensburg players who are all trying desperately to punch the ball loose from his grip. Tim knowingly protects the ball with both hands, fights for every step, shakes off one of the tacklers, and drags two with him as he falls.

His hand, gripping the football, appears to just break the goal line. Both sets of coaches on the sidelines are staring at Tim, the football, exactly where they both went down, and the referee.

The black and white shirted line ref is right there, crouched down, watching closely, and sees that the firmly-held ball broke the plane of the goal line before his knee touched, and he stands, shooting both arms up in the air, signaling...

"TOUCHDOWN!!! Lake Luzerne just scored a last-second clutch touchdown!" is uncontrollably squealed by the radio DJ.

The ecstatically blown-away Lake Luzerne coaches, who are all jumping up and down with their arms in the air—along with the team and the entire Lake Luzerne bleachers full of fans—all come screaming onto the field.

Timmy gets up, spikes the ball hard, and immediately gets slammed into and hugged by an emotional Eddie, and seconds later, the entire team.

Samantha, so proud of her younger brother, Eddie, and his best friend, turns to look at the scoreboard and sees Lake Luzerne 19, Warrensburg 14, and the clock reading 00:00.

Butch looks at Samantha and says, "We got us a brand new football team!" Butch and Samantha remember last season when the Wolverines trounced them 28 to 0.

Up in the booth, the radio DJ puts his hand over his mic and asks his statistics guy, "Who the heck was that? Who lateraled the ball and who scored that touchdown for Lake Luzerne?"

The young man nervously fumbles with some papers, finds the roster, and quickly points out the names. The radio DJ nods his head, uncovers his mic, and says, "Folks, we just witnessed a brilliant defensive takeaway! Number forty-four, Eddie Barone, created the fumble and ran sixty yards before being tackled by number twelve, Bad Brad Rivas! Before Eddie hit the ground, he lateraled the ball to number twenty-nine, Tim Carswell a defensive tackle, who fought off three Warrensburg players, taking two with him over the goal line, and scored a touchdown! Eddie and Tim are both first-year starters on the defensive squad! Wow, ladies and gentlemen, just...WOW! What a play and what a turn-around!"

The stats guy then hands the DJ a news article about Eddie Barone getting a commendation from the New York State Governor for bravery above and beyond.

Justin Bao is driving, listening to his radio, and screaming, "Touchdown! With no seconds left on the clock!" And as he listens to the radio further, he says, "Eddie lateraled the ball to Timmy, and Timmy dragged the whole freakin' team over the goal line with him! Yeah! The kid's a steamroller! Go Eagles!"

Also listening on her Tahoe's radio was Police Chief Nancy Rector, who really wanted to be at the game but whose posted work schedule—especially if you're the Chief—needs to be honored. She cannot help thinking, *Two former bullies, who I sent to juvenile hall, have turned over a new leaf, and a very big positive leaf at that.*

"A great achievement today and a proud moment for them, their parents, and their coaches. What a great transition! And Marty-Bull had hugged him." Justin says to himself with a very content, knowing look on his face.

Nan calls Lisa Barone, Eddie's mom, because she knows Lisa will be at the game with the Carswell's.

Lisa has her smart phone in her hand. When it rings, she sees who the call is from and immediately answers with, "Hi, Nan."

Nan says, "Wow, that turnaround was incredible! Please give my congratulations to Eddie and to Tim and his parents. Great game!"

Lisa replies, "Thanks so much, Nan! All I want to do is hug him, and I can't even get close." She laughs, so happy and so proud of her son and his best friend, the Carswell's youngest boy, whom she has known since he was born.

Over the loud speaker system, the radio DJ says, "Great defensive plays by Tim Carswell and Eddie Barone are what made the difference in today's game. By the way, Eddie, congratulations on getting that commendation for bravery from the Governor! Your community is a better place because of you!"

Eddie and Tim, arm in arm, are both hopping up and down with the number one finger in the air as their team-mates and the crowd follow them back to the sidelines chanting, "Ea-gles!, Ea-gles!..."

The Warrensburg Wolverines and their Coaches are coming across the field to congratulate their Lake Luzerne opponents. After the game, the teams, win or lose, both get in two big lines and shake hands. "As upset as you are at losing Carlton, it's just one game…and we will get them next time," says his Head Coach.

Chapter Six

"Describe Them?"

At the football game, unbeknownst to the crowd of well-wishing fans, two middle-aged men, who were in the bleachers and who did not take part in the celebration, walk to their dark gray SUV in the parking lot. A large, broad-shouldered, heavily tattooed male with a closely cropped black beard, wearing a baseball cap and sunglasses, gets out and is standing next to the car waiting for them. He opens the back doors, and they get in. One of the men puts a Nikon camera with a high-power 500mm telephoto lens on the seat between them.

"Okay, we know what Eddie 'Mr. Commendation for Bravery' Barone looks like; now let's go get an oil change and see where Todd Stearns hangs out."

Moments later in town, the SUV slows down and stops in the street off to the side of the repair shop. Armando, from the driver's seat, scans the auto repair shop with a set of binoculars. After ten seconds, he says, "No surveillance—not even a Ring doorbell; nada."

One of the guys in the back seat says, "Good ol' American small town trust. Now I see why Henry chose these towns."

The other guy chimes in, "Yeah, Henry the rat."

They pull up and park right in front of the open garage doors. There is a sign overhead that says, "Please do not park in front of the garage doors." They see Terry, and one of the guys asks him, "Hey, amigo, can you do a quick oil change?"

Terry notices his thick accent, and he also notices the T&LC (Taxi & Limousine Commission) designation on the license plate and wonders, "Why would they want to change the oil in a rented limousine service, brand new SUV that obviously has a driver?" *Hmm, more like a bodyguard from the looks of him,* he thinks as he smiles back at them without tipping his hand.

Both electric lifts have vehicles on them, and all the wheels have been removed for brake jobs. Terry points at the two lifts and says, "Complete brake jobs, and on that one," he points, "I need to replace the lines. Monday afternoon is the soonest I can do an oil change, fellas. You can try the Sunoco Station in Queensbury. I can give you directions." He basically gets ignored as the three men walk closer, looking around the shop.

"Hey, you work on bicycles too."

After an agonizing ten minutes with these three suspiciously strange men, Terry, who had memorized their license plate number just to make sure, writes it down after they drive out of sight and thinks to himself, *I need to go see Police Chief Nan.* Twenty minutes later, he is at the police station.

"Can you describe what these men looked like, Terry?"

"Describe them?" he asks and chuckles. "After Henry's arrest, I installed hidden video cameras all over the business and the home. I could point the little cameras out to you, and you still wouldn't see them."

He sets his weekly bank deposit bag on her desk, ruffles through a number of checks, pulls out a DVD, and hands it to Nan, who immediately pops it into her computer. "This will show you exactly, in high-resolution full color, who paid my son and me a visit today."

They watch for a minute, and then Nan says, "Huh, the resolution is great, Terry. I think I can even make out their license plate number." Nan is squinting at the video.

Terry hands her a piece of paper with the license plate number on it and says, "I was worried about that, so, just in case, here it is."

"Wow, this is great! I am going to copy and email this DVD to Carla, okay?"

"Absolutely," Terry replies.

Five minutes later, U.S. Attorney for the Northern District, Carla Williams, calls Nan and requests, "Can we do a Zoom meeting in... say, fifteen minutes? That will give me time to round up Gary and watch the video with him."

Like clockwork, fifteen minutes later, there is Carla and FBI Special Agent in Charge, Gary Rogers, on one end and Terry and Nan on the other.

Carla says, "Hi, Terry, nice to meet you." Gary waves. Terry and Nan wave back.

Carla continues. "We are getting ready to act on what Henry told us. This is perfect timing. On your video are two of the cartel leaders' sons, Serafin and Ismael, who literally are in charge of North America. The big guy with them is Armando, their body guard and lead enforcer."

Agent Rogers adds, "I thought for sure that after we arrested Henry, they would have left the country. But here they are in Lake Luzerne. Just pure arrogance."

Carla looks directly at Terry Stearns via computer screen and asks him, "Okay, let's start. Your name is Terrence Stearns and you reside in the town of Lake Luzerne, New York. Todd Stearns is your son. Is this correct?"

"Yes, it is correct," Terry replies.

"Is what you are about to say on this video recorded conversation true and factual, of your own free will and without coercion, intimidation, or threat of retaliation?"

"Yes, one-hundred percent," Terry replies.

"You also acknowledge and agree that I, U.S. Attorney, Carla Williams, FBI Agent Gary Rogers, or anyone else for that matter have not exerted any undue pressure or influence on you in this regard."

"Yes, I acknowledge and agree," Terry replies.

"Did you record and do you exclusively own the video sent to me today by Police Chief Nancy Rector, and are you willing to turn it over to the U.S. Attorney's office as State's evidence?" Carla asks.

"Yes," Terry replies.

"Okay Terry, why did you go to your local police station today?" Carla asks.

"Today around 4 p.m., my son Todd and I were visited at our place of business by the three men on the video. They were not anyone I knew or had ever seen before, and we—my son and I—both felt intimidated. Frankly, my wife and I have had a number of sleepless nights since the Henry incident involving my son Todd happened. "Did these men say anything to you that made you feel threatened?" Carla asks.

"They didn't have to say anything. They were joking around, acting like we were best friends from high school, until...the guy in the yellow-tinted aviator sunglasses walked back to see Todd in his bike shop. I didn't like this and said, 'Hey, where are you going? You can't just walk into my shop,' and that is when the big, tattooed guy took off his sunglasses so I could see his eyes and blocked me while the other one was behind me telling me how important it was that I do an oil change on his... rented SUV? It was complete BS, and I thought they would harm my son and me if I tried to stop them.

"Anyway, after a few seconds, I was ready to go after him no matter what, and the guy came strolling back into my side of the shop. He said thank you and they left. Todd immediately came out of his bike shop and asked me, 'Who was that guy? He was creepy!' That was when I downloaded the DVD, locked the shop up, took Todd home to his mom—who is a full-on Mama Bear—and came here to see Nan…uhh, Police Chief Rector."

Gary says, "The oil change was their rouse to get a foot in the door. They own that SUV, and they own the limo and rental car company the SUV came from. Just like they own the rental car Henry was arrested in, just one of the many things they do."

Carla adds, "The cartel owns the corporations, but the individual companies are partially owned and operated by squeaky-clean individuals that are paid to look the other way. Legally it's a nightmare, but with Henry's testimony we will leverage these so-called squeaky clean operators to tell us the truth or face the consequences."

Police Chief Nan says, "All because of four brave kids…and we need to protect them."

Carla replies, "All because of four brave kids and a police department that was one hundred percent on top of the situation, and we WILL protect them; that is a promise!"

After a brief moment of silence. "Any questions for me?" asks Carla.

Terry looks at Nan and then at Carla, and says, "I'm good."

"Thank you for coming forward, Terry. I am confident you and your family will never see any of those people ever again. Police Chief Rector, always a pleasure. Gotta go, lots to do here."

As the Zoom screen fades to black Terry stands, goes to shake Nan's hand, and she hauls off and hugs her old friend that she attended elementary school with. "So proud of you, Terry."

Ten minutes after the Zoom meeting, her administrator flies into the room and hands Carla five documents freshly signed by a Federal Judge, of which three are new arrest warrants.

That same Federal Judge, who watched Terry's high-resolution video in his office upstairs, instantly recognized the brothers, and, from an undisclosed sign-in, watched the Zoom meeting in its entirety. *Carla, God bless her, is taking the proverbial bull by the horns,* thinks the judge, admiring her greatly.

She co-signs the documents, makes two sets of copies, puts the originals and a copy in a briefcase, and hands them to FBI Special Agent Gary Rogers.

"Well, here you go. If driving a company vehicle all the way from New York City to Lake Luzerne to get an oil change and then having Armando the Beast block his path as one of the brother's talks to his minor son isn't intimidating a potential witness, I do not know what is. You are right, Gary. Pure arrogance."

Gary responds with, "And they would treat Terry like they were best friends from high school... right up until he and his son disappeared off this planet."

Carla nods her head in recognition and goes right back to the business at hand, continuing with, "In this briefcase is the state-wide BOLO for three armed and extremely dangerous men and a search and seizure for the Lincoln SUV or whatever vehicle they are in at the time of arrest.

Let's get them before they get back to the city. It's a four-hour drive, and they have a two-hour head start. You also have separate and specific no-knock search warrants for the limo and rental car premises, all vehicles, any adjacent or related properties, all phones, computers, their personal homes and rental homes in New York, New Jersey, and Connecticut, plus the offices, hangars, and planes at four airports, and a total of fifty-seven felony arrest warrants. Our number one priority is to rescue the children and anyone else they are holding captive. This video… is the icing on the Henry cake."

"The FBI has been waiting for this moment for a very long time. This is by far the largest task force I have ever worked with—eighty-six field agents along with multi-jurisdictional police and SWAT teams from three states."

"Go get em' Gary!"

"Thanks for everything, Carla."

Gary walks out the door, and she sits back in her chair, closes her eyes, and takes a deep breath, slowly exhaling. "And thank you, Lake Luzerne," she whispers to her now quiet inner office, whose walls are covered with polished dark reddish brown hardwood cases full of leather-bound law books.

The thick wood and glass soundproof door opens, and Gary briskly walks out of Carla's side office. To the team of five guardedly-optimistic, wide-eyed agents jumping to their feet as soon as they see him, he says, "We got the big green light—all of it!" He lifts and pats the briefcase. "Let's GO!"

Between the U.S. attorney's private waiting area—which, thankfully, has a coffee maker—and their manned vehicles parked right out front, seventeen phone calls are made by three of the agents, delivering the same long-awaited message, "Let's go!" The entire elated task force in three states jumps to their feet, high-fives, and gears up.

Gary and the other two senior field agents take the elevator to the roof and board an awaiting FBI helicopter soon to be in pursuit of the gray Lincoln SUV. The helicopter cruises at 160 miles per hour. Gary immediately calls the Captain of the NY State Police for an update. *The FBI is not playing around either.*

Thirty minutes later, high-tech video surveillance cameras on the FBI helicopter and the state police pursuit vehicle capture a gloved hand throwing one, two, three, four, and then a fifth handgun out the back seat window of the speeding SUV into the grass on the side of the interstate highway.

Gary laughs. "It just gets better and better!"

Chapter Seven

"What Is Gefilte Fish?"

Six months have passed and it's now time for the annual April 22nd carp bow fishing derby at Canadarago Lake in Richfield Springs, NY, a two hour drive from Lake Luzerne. Meyer Kravitz, the local kosher Deli owner, who will turn the carp into gefilte fish, is standing with Justin, Nate, Nate's Dad Jesse Coleman, who is one of Meyer's oldest friends, and then we have Mike, Butch and Danny Frasier. Wayne and Becky both politely declined to go because they simply do not hunt or fish.

Danny asks Meyer the Deli owner, "Mr. Kravitz, what is gefilte fish?"

Meyer responds with, "Ahhhh, gefilte fish is a staple of East European Jewish cooking. Without gefilte fish, a holiday is not a holiday! Gefilte fish literally means stuffed fish, which is ground up fish mixed with eggs, bread or matza crumbs which I prefer, *secret* spices, salt, onions, carrots, and sometimes potatoes, to produce a fish ball which is then simmered in fish stock and garnished with a slice of carrot on top, and another *secret* horseradish mixture on the side called chrain. Dee-licious!"

Nate adds, "And you have THE best Deli, Meyer. For years now!" And then to the group he says, "This all started when I was a kid. My Dad and I would come up from Florida to our camp here on the lake and one Spring he taught me how to bowfish for carp. In the beginning it was just the two of us and over time turned into this derby. Otsego, Onondaga and Oneida Lakes have lots of carp as well and also have Spring time derbies. The carp love to eat other fish eggs and if there are a lot of carp, whole populations of game fish in the lake are threatened. No game fish means fewer summer people, fewer cabin rentals, fewer restaurant and antique store visits, etc., ergo the derbies. Dad would shoot the carp from our flat bottomed rowboat with his bow. His arrows were attached to a fishing line on a pole I was holding and I'd reel them in. Let me tell ya, reeling in a twenty pound carp is no easy task."

His Dad, Jesse, a true historian of the sport, continues with, "Common carp are fun to catch because they do get big and put up a heck of a fight. Originally from Asia, carp were first introduced into New York State waters in 1831 to provide people with another food fish. The current state record carp is 50 pounds 6 ounces, and was caught from the Tomhannock Reservoir in Rensselaer County. While the likelihood of us encountering a carp of that size here is low, the lakes around here are abundant with carp in the 10-30 pound range.

So, seeing how there are six of us we need to split up into two-man teams. The team with the total combined weight of the five heaviest fish wins the tourney and a $500.00 cash prize. That is why there is a $25 entry fee. Each boat will get between fifteen and twenty carp, so that means around four hundred trout and bass egg-eating carp could be removed from the lake today. Any questions?"

"Nope," is the aggregate response from the group.

"Okay, now this is important. For every foot of depth between the fish and the water's surface, you need to aim six inches BELOW your target. These carp are going to be in about three feet of water, so aim the arrow a good foot-and-a-half below the fish. Got it?"

Everyone replies, "Got it."

Jesse continues with, "So, teams. How about me and Danny, Nate and Butch, and Justin and Mike?"

"I have bow fished before; how about you, Justin?" asks Mike.

"I can't say I have, but I can reel one in," replies Justin. Justin thinks to himself, *I wish I had brought Newton. He could have probably talked the carp into coming to the boat. No, Newton would never do that. I can just hear him, all upset, 'You shot that fish!'*

Jesse continues with, "As soon as they blow the air horn"—he looks at his watch—"which should be in five minutes, we jump in the boat, turn the speed control on the trolling motor tiller all the way counterclockwise, and head out to that"—Jesse points—"corner of the lake, which is the shallow inlet where the ice has melted and the sun has warmed up the water. But don't fall in; it's cold, and you will muddy up the very clear water." He looks at his son, Nate. Nate looks back at his dad and chuckles, remembering just such an event.

The horn blows! Jesse and Danny hop into their boat, and Jesse turns the handle on the tiller of the electric trolling motor. Jesse's boat is in the front of the boat pack because he is the honorary founder of the event.

On the way over to the spot, Jesse hands Danny the bow, and he takes the fishing pole. It's one of the only old-fashioned setups, but that's the way Jesse likes it.

Jesse explains, "When we get there, remember to keep the arrow eighteen inches below the target, and try to keep the arrow at a 45-degree angle and hit the carp broadside. That angle gives you the most available target space."

Danny listens to every word and replies, "Okay... The 45-degree angle will be about eight feet away from the boat."

Jesse smiles and says, "One hundred percent correct, young man!"

Danny nocks a metal fishing arrow into the compound bow and tests the pull strength.

Jesse backs off on the speed and rests the trolling motor at an angle as it slowly circles. He stands and says, "Okay, here we are."

As Jesse scans the shallows towards the shore, Danny is looking on the other side of the boat. He asks, "Whoa. Is that what I think it is?"

Jesse looks to where Danny is pointing and says, "It sure is, and it's a big one. Take your time. Follow it."

Danny does just that, slowly exhales, shoots, and then the line on the fishing reel goes zing, zing, *ziiiiing*. Jesse grabs it and clicks on the drag, and the line still goes zing, *ziiiing,* but now the rod is bent. Jesse hands Danny the rod and reel, takes the bow, and the fight begins.

"Wow-zah! Danny got one! A big one!" yells Butch.

"Go Danny!" yells his dad, Mike.

Arrows are being shot. Mike misses his first one, and so does Butch, but some of the local lake veterans are hitting their targets.

Nate calmly tells Butch the same thing his dad told him over and over: "Take your time, Butch, follow it... Squat down a little for that 45-degree angle."

Butch does, and this time he hits the carp. Nate's modern bow has the reel attached to it, so Butch grabs it and starts cranking the carp back to the boat, but the carp keeps taking line.

"Wow, they sure do fight!" Nate says. "Set the drag just a little tighter but let them run. We do not want him to break the line and take off with our arrow."

Jesse hauls Danny's fish into the boat, pulls the arrow, and takes a photo of Danny and his first big carp. One of the locals in a nearby boat sees it and says, "Hey Jesse, your boy there just might have the biggest one of the day. That's an easy twenty pounder."

"Twenty-five!" Jesse says with a big smile. Danny, likewise, is smiling ear-to-ear. "Oh yeah, this is a big fish Mr. Coleman! Thanks!"

With close to twenty boats on the lake, at the end of the day, Meyer Kravitz goes home with over one hundred pounds of filets from derby donors. The Kravitz family always contributes trays of sandwiches and hors d'oeuvres to the Canadarago Lake Improvement Association's fund-raising summer chili cook-off and pie-making event, so this is a win-win for everyone.

Chapter Eight

"Look Out - Here We Come!"

A week or so later, the sun is rising on a brisk mountain spring morning, and Justin and Grace are sitting on their back deck overlooking Lake George, having coffee. The ice has receded off the shoreline, and the shallows are teeming with fish happy to be in the sunlit clear and warmer water.

Justin looks at his wife, sees that certain thoughtful look in her eyes, and does not interrupt. After a moment, Grace turns, looks at Justin, and smiles. "I was thinking about seeing Rohan and his herd up at Lake Tear. He reminds me of someone I know—strong, kind, and smart." She winks at him. What's nice is that Justin knows she means it. There's no hidden agenda with Grace; she speaks her mind, and that's it.

Justin smiles back, appreciating his dear, wonderful Grace on every level. "I would love to see Loki and Iostha again. A pack of timber wolves in New York State that no one knows exists except us. They can smell a human from a mile away. No one is ever going to see them unless they want you to."

"Dad said we are going back as soon as the snow melts. That's this month. Maybe Loki and Iostha will be back in Beaver Town," she chuckles.

Justin laughs. "Ha. There sure are a lot of beavers there." He finishes his coffee and asks, "How's your day looking?"

Grace replies, "Otto is going to his forever home today. He is such a good boy. Nice couple, three young kids, big yard. They fostered him a week ago, brought him back on the scheduled day, and are coming back to get him. They told me that they all missed him terribly after he was gone. You know who missed him the most? Their cat, Smoky! That huge German Shepherd and a Russian Blue are best friends."

"Nice. Gotta love those odd couples who have so much in common," he says, winking back at Grace, who gives him a cute smirk in return.

Spring has indeed sprung in the beautiful Adirondack Mountains of Upstate New York. Most of the snow has melted, and fresh, crisp vernal pools have once again filled up with water and salamander eggs. Behind Newton's Pond, it's been two long weeks. They laid their egg ball in the quite large vernal pool with the downed tree laying across it—the very same pool where Wayne first encountered the aquatic phase green newt with the curious red dots on its sides. He had never seen one before, so he took one home to show Grandpa, who knew exactly what it was. Grandpa, seeing the gentle fascination in Wayne's eyes, knew it was time for him to meet his old friend, Newton.

After swimming across their pond and taking a short walk, Newton and Janine anxiously swim out to check on their egg ball. It could be gone as far as they know, eaten by predators, but most likely it will be a cluster of thirty to forty small eggs, in part protected by the vernal pool that will have no fish.

As they swim closer, they are happy to see that the egg ball is still there, and then... Newton's eyes announce his astonishment! There are not only one but two big eggs, and they are huge!

Under the water, Newton, beyond stunned, tells Janine, "As far as I know, this has never happened before. Every ancient newt that can communicate with humans has come from a big egg, and sometimes years and years go by without one. It took me over seventy years to finally find you." Janine looks lovingly back at Newton and blushes.

Once back on land at their home, Newton looks up at the tree and yells, "Grubbins?" He sticks his head out of his home, and Newton says, "Can you go get Wayne and Becky? It's important." Grubbins immediately takes flight.

Janine says, "Your mom and dad have to come back to our pond from Lake Tear of the Clouds to witness the birth."

Newton nods and remembers how his parents got back home with Grandpa Perkins and the scary—yet amazing—helicopter ride with their beaver family. He also thinks back on Grandpa's surprising tribal dance and song with the eagles celebrating them—their constant, loving protectors in the sky.

"Oh my, Janine, these eggs are huge!" Newton exclaims, still stunned and bewildered.

Janine, also shell-shocked, looks back at Newton with happy amazement and says, "She spoke to me, Newton. I heard her little voice in my head."

Newton gasps and says, "Oh, my. Wayne and Becky should be here soon, and my folks really need to see this…wait—what did she say to you?" Newton is now wondering why he did not hear her voice as well.

Janine squints down, thinking, and replies, "It was in the old language... the way a baby newt would understand it. Basically, she said, "Look out, here we come!"

"*Ohhh* my!" Newton exhales, nervous and excited at the same time.

The End

$$<<<<<<<<\diamond>>>>>>>>$$

Last Visited: 05/23/23 at 07:53am

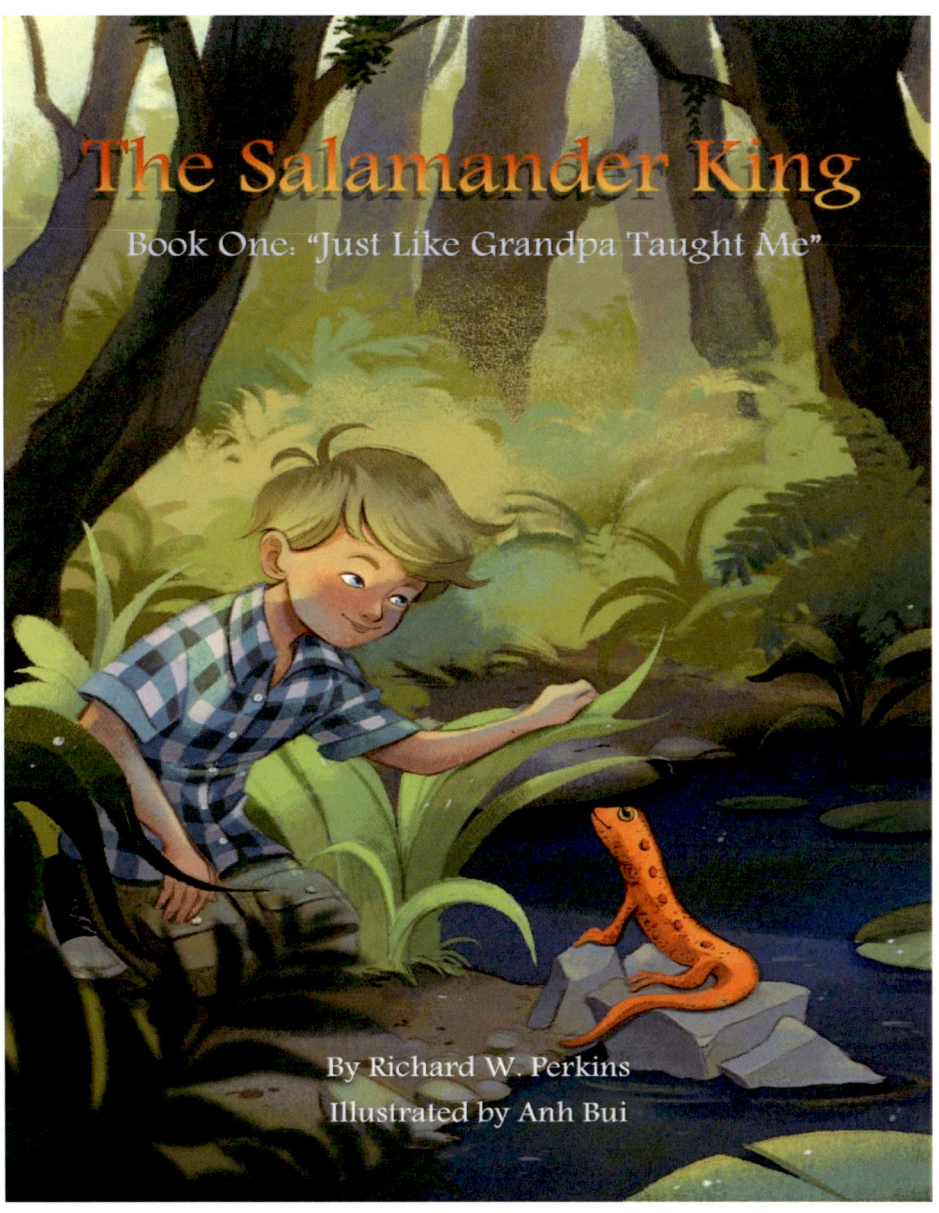

Book One is available on Amazon.com and at select bookstores. In Book One, loving and caring for animals that others find insignificant, and the difference between right and wrong, is knowledge I want to pass on... just like Grandpa taught me in Lake Luzerne, NY all those years ago.

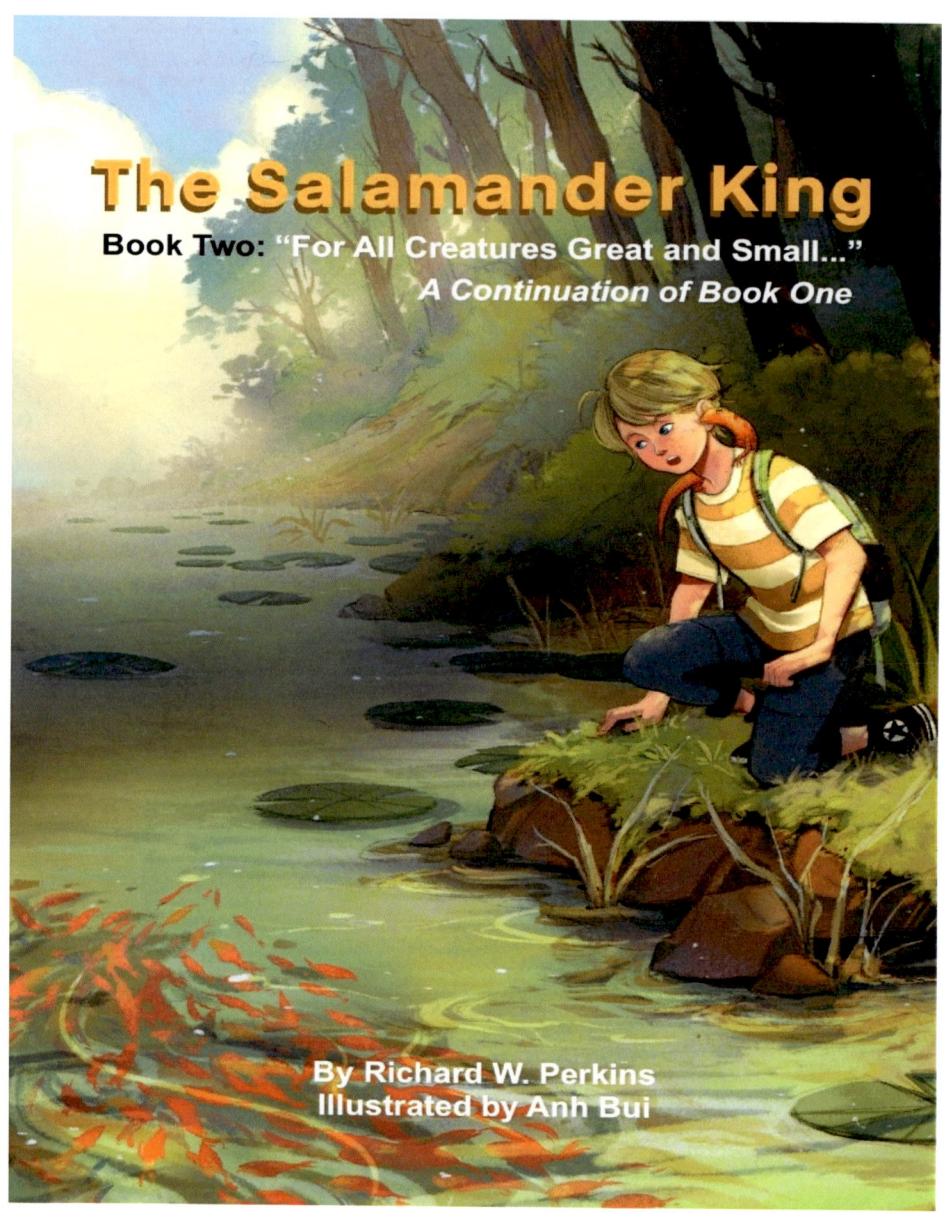

The Salamander King

Book Two: "For All Creatures Great and Small..."
A Continuation of Book One

By Richard W. Perkins
Illustrated by Anh Bui

   Book Two is available on Amazon.com and at select bookstores. Here comes amazing eleven-year-old Becky. The overall theme is, "You do not have to be a lion... to be important to others." Becky's dad, the new Vet in town, agrees when he saves Marty-Bull the beaver, who was shot with an arrow after warning Wayne and Becky. For all creatures great and small, love and caring conquers all.

The Salamander King

Book Three: "We Have Found Our New Minnie"

A Continuation of Books One and Two...

Written By: Richard W. Perkins
Illustrated By: Dibyoshree Sarkar

Book Three is available on Amazon.com and at select bookstores. In Book Three, the kids deal with feral dogs, stolen endangered newts, and girl bullies, who—according to my sister and many other young ladies I have spoken with—are just as bad as the boys! And…we have found our new Minnie!

The Salamander King
Book Four: *"Let's Go!"*

Written By: Richard W. Perkins
Illustrated By: Dibyoshree Sarkar

A Continuation of Books One thru Three

Book Four is available on Amazon.com and at select bookstores. Newton goes back to his birthplace, Lake Tear of the Clouds, in search of his parents where he finds so much more. And, oh-oh, how is Wayne going to get out from underneath that submerged log?!

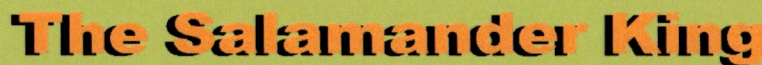

The Salamander King

Book Five: *"As Absurd As That Sounds..."*

A Direct Continuation of Books One thru Four

Written By: Richard W. Perkins
Illustrated By: Dibyoshree Sarkar

Book Five is available on Amazon.com and at select bookstores. Wayne and Becky get involved in wild animal rescue, learn about salamander physiology, and discover that bullies can change for the better. And then…Wayne goes to do a good deed for a visiting vacationer and gets abducted! Becky is with him. Will she get abducted too?

Contact the Author via email: perkinsphoto7@aol.com

or mail: BKBP, 82 Lincoln Street, Bath, Maine 04530

An ongoing story about a very smart salamander, friends,

family, a fragile pond and…bullies!

Book Seven is coming soon!

Great Grandpa Donald Lidell Whitmore's map, passed down to his son, Lynn, and now to his great-grandson, Wayne, all three Salamander King's.

Milton Keynes UK
Ingram Content Group UK Ltd.
UKRC031937290923
429674UK00006B/95